Mwah Mwah

Other titles by Chloë Rayban from Bloomsbury

Drama Queen

Featuring Hollywood Bliss

My Life Starring Mum

Hollywood Bliss – My Life So Far

Mwah Mwah

Chloë Rayban

BLOOMSBURY

LONDON BERLIN NEW YORK

First published in Great Britain in 2008 by Bloomsbury Publishing Plc
36 Soho Square, London, W1D 3QY

A CIP catalogue record of this book is available from the British Library

ISBN 978 0 7475 9413 0

Typeset by RefineCatch Limited, Bungay, Suffolk
Printed in Great Britain by Clays Ltd, St Ives Plc

5 7 9 10 8 6 4

www.bloomsbury.com

FSC
Mixed Sources
Product group from well-managed
forests and other controlled sources
Cert no. SGS-COC-2061
www.fsc.org
© 1996 Forest Stewardship Council

The paper this book is printed on is certified independently in accordance with the rules of the FSC.
It is ancient-forest friendly. The printer holds chain of custody.

For Claudia, who became the perfect Parisienne

Chapter One

'Mayjesweesewer.   Annaseraravy!   Weegrobeezoo. Abeeantow.'

Mum put down the phone and turned to me with a delighted smile.

'That was Marie-Christine!'

'I'd never've guessed.'

'She's invited you to stay with Matthilde for the Easter holidays!'

'What!'

'In Paris. You'll love it.'

'Mum! I will NOT love it. Not with Matthilde. She's so . . . uggghhhrr.'

Mum frowned. 'So *what*?'

'Well, like, so *French*!'

'Nonsense. I know you didn't exactly hit it off the last time you met, but you were only . . . eight?'

'Ten, actually. She was twelve, going on eighteen.'

'Anyway, it's all been decided. They're expecting you on Friday.'

'Friday! Why Friday?'

'It's the day I have to leave for that conference in Amsterdam, so it fits in perfectly.'

'Oh, I get it now. This is just somewhere to dump me.'

'No. It's a wonderful opportunity to improve your French.'

'I don't want to improve my French. I keep telling you, I'd rather do Spanish.'

Mum got up and made for the kitchen as if the conversation had come to an end. I followed her. She bent down, totally ignoring me, taking things out of the tumble dryer as if her life depended on it.

'It might interest you to know, I've got things planned for the Easter holidays. I can stay with Jess.'

'You know what your father and I think about Jessica.'

'What's wrong with her?'

'Last time I saw her, she was smoking in the street. *And* she had a lip-ring.'

'It wasn't a real lip-ring, it was a clip on. And where else are you supposed to smoke these days?'

'Hannah!'

'Mum, listen, I *don't* want to go to France. I'm going to miss loads. Everyone's going to Angie's this Saturday. Her dad's hired a proper DJ's deck and everything.'

Mum put down the T-shirt she was folding and stared at me. 'You can't mean you'd miss out on a trip to Paris for the sake of a *party*.'

'Yes, as a matter of fact. I hate France, you know I do.'

'But you haven't even *been* to Paris.'

'It's full of posey people. Everyone says so.'

'But you'll love it at the Poiriers' – they've got a really stylish apartment.'

'You mean they live in a *flat*?'

Mum ignored me. She lifted the pile of folded washing and headed up the stairs. I was hard on her heels.

'I'm nearly fourteen and I've got a life of my own,' I growled at her back. 'You can't make me go.'

Mum paused at her bedroom door and turned to me with a fixed expression. 'I didn't think I'd have to.'

'Well, I'm not going and that's that.' I stomped into my room and slammed the door. Hard.

Parents! They think they own you. Just because, by some random freak of nature, you happen to be born to them, rather than someone else – someone reasonable, generous and understanding – they think they have a right to control your life! Mum loves France, therefore I have to love France. Just because she took a degree in French and spent her one 'dream' year at Grenoble University where she shared a flat with Marie-Christine and where they got *welded at the hip*! Ugghhhrrr, *Marie-Christine*. The minute they're together, Mum switches from being a nice normal English person to this strange kind of witch whose mouth goes in convulsions and comes out with pure gobble-de-gook. And Matthilde is a mini Marie-Christine in the making!

I thought back to that last time we met. While Marie-Christine and Mum were laughing like hyenas in the kitchen at some gobble-de-joke of theirs, Matthilde and I were sent to 'play together' in my bedroom. Without a word being spoken – well, naturally, since neither of us spoke the other's language – Matthilde instantly took charge. She found a pack of cards and tried to teach me the world's most boring and unintelligible game, in which she always won. Or at least I think she did because she looked so incredibly pleased with herself. Then she went to sit with the grown-ups and joined in their conversation and drank a little cup of their black coffee, making it all too clear she thought playing with me was way below her dignity. Uggghhhrrr! And to think that Mum is expecting me to spend my precious Easter holidays with *them*.

I had other plans – which had to do with Angie's party, actually – only four more days to go! Plans which included a boy who Angie's brother knew, called Mark. Not that I was really interested in him or anything. But he *had* almost asked me out. At least he'd asked me whether I liked Jackie Chan. And since I hadn't actually ever seen a Jackie Chan movie and didn't want to admit it, I said I could take him or leave him. At which he said, 'Pity, because there's a movie of his coming to the Odeon on Thursday.' I still get a sinking feeling remembering the back of his head as he walked away. If only, if only I hadn't said that. However, knowing my luck, if I'd raved about Jackie Chan, he probably would've said he was rubbish.

Anyway, I was going to put all that right at Angie's party. I'd double-checked that Mark was coming. I'd been preparing carefully for this event. I had a new strappy top, my best-fitting straight-leg jeans were washed and pressed ready under a pile of books, and those boots I managed to persuade Mum to buy me were still lying untouched in their box. I'd even got a couple of Jackie Chan movies out of the video shop by way of research. I was right – I can take him or leave him. However, I guess kung fu movies are more of a boy-thing really and it doesn't mean Mark and I are fundamentally incompatible. In fact, I'm sure we're not. The minute I set eyes on him I knew instinctively that Mark and I were ideal boyfriend and girlfriend material. So this Saturday was going to be the beginning of a totally new life for me. Coupledom!!! That is, *if I don't get packed off to Paris.*

I've been packed off to Paris. I'm standing behind all these people lining up with their bags and kids and grandmas and whatever, waiting to check in for Flight 8674 to Paris CDG. Dad backed Mum up. He said the experience would be 'character-forming'. Personally, I think my character is pretty well formed already. Normally, I have my own opinions and make my own decisions. Having to give in to parents is a step in the wrong direction if you ask me.

'Are you all right, dear?' asked the 'kind lady' who was queuing for the X-ray machine in front of me. I could have killed Mum. At thirteen and three-quarters I am perfectly able to get on a plane, for godsake. But she had to tap this woman on the shoulder who she just happened to notice had the same check in-time on her ticket, and ask her if she wouldn't mind 'keeping an eye' on me.

Mum made off after that, said she had an 'important meeting', but I reckon in actual fact she wanted to get rid of me before I could have more of a moan at her.

Going through security is like tenth degree. I actually have my can of Diet Coke confiscated and what precisely do they expect to find in my shoes? Once I'm through to the departure lounge, the place is heaving with people. There are monitors with loads of other flights going to Paris, which is just the teensiest bit confusing, so I'm sticking like glue to the 'kind lady' who seems to know her way around. But she's spotted WHSmith's and has taken it into her head to buy a newspaper. I trail behind her as she selects her paper and joins a queue to pay for it, which is so long, it snakes all the way through the shop and out the other end. There must be about eighty people in front of us. The queue is edging forward at about one person every fifty seconds. I start doing some extremely complicated maths, trying to estimate how many minutes it will take to get to the cash desk and whether this purchase of the *Daily Telegraph* will mean we'll miss Flight 8674 and never get to Paris. Ten minutes, which feel like half a lifetime, scroll by. I start giving the 'kind lady' meaningful glances.

She catches one of them. 'You go on ahead, dear, if you like. Gate C11. I'll see you there.'

I swallow. 'Right. OK.'

I locate a sign pointing to Gates C10–25 and start out in that direction. I follow hordes of people down an escalator and through a corridor on to a moving walkway. Once on the walkway I'm wondering frantically if I've missed a sign somewhere and am being swept helplessly in the wrong direction. An endless corridor takes me past umpteen other gates. Gate C11 seems to have been spirited away to the very far end of the airport. I can feel my hands going sweaty with panic. At this rate I may well be walking to Paris.

But at last I spot the mythical letters C11 and standing at a desk beneath them is a nice helpful flight person, who checks my ticket and confirms I'm in the right place. I sink into a seat feeling rather pleased with myself.

Grudgingly, I have to admit this is a bit of an adventure. Of course, I've been to France before, loads of times, but always in the car with Dad and Mum. Mainly because they seem to think France is the only place where you can have a decent holiday. Other people foolishly fly off to hotels in countries that are too hot or too crowded or too horribly commercialised while we always drive to some slightly damp rented house in Normandy, which is called a gîte. We've stayed in countless gîtes; they can be crumbling cottages or spanking new bungalows, buried in the country or sand-blasted by the beach, but fundamentally they're all the same. They all have that very particular gîte smell – an evil mixture of calor gas and loo freshener. And strange patterned plasticised tablecloths that smell of sick. And garden chairs that collapse under you and a table with one wonky leg. They have pillows stuffed with something festering and lumpy and their showers douse you with water that's either icy cold or scalding hot, never in-between.

By the time I've finished this resentful catalogue of memories a muffled voice over a loudspeaker is saying something about 'proceeding directly to gate number C11' and everyone around me is shuffling to their feet. I join the queue, wondering what has happened to the 'kind lady'. At this rate she'd have been better off with me keeping an eye on her. But as my ticket and passport is checked, I spot her running down the corridor to join the very far end of the queue, waving her *Daily Telegraph* at me.

About half an hour or so later we have flown over the Channel. Nice normal dependable England has been left behind and foreign unpredictable France is spread out beneath us. We've all had to wind our watches on an hour, because in France they don't even stick to the same time as us. In their typical posey competitive way, they have to be one hour ahead. At this point, I remember Angie's party tomorrow and experience another wave of suppressed fury over how I've been sent off like this *against my will.* I sit mentally listing all the negatives I have about the French.

Negative 1.   They're not to be trusted — all that fake politeness and charm. All that mwah-mwah kissing on both cheeks.

Negative 2.   They're rude. Think of the way French waiters treat you.

Negative 3.   Too chic to be true. They seem to think they invented fashion.

Negative 4.   They're snooty. All that fuss about haute cuisine and haute couture, and blooming Club 'Méd-it-erra-née'.

Negative 5.   They're immoral. According to French movies, all married men have lovers.

Negative 6.   They're cruel. They shoot every-thing on sight — then eat it.

Negative 7.   They're totally weird about food anyway — committed carnivores who eat totally gross stuff like brains and ears and tails. I mean, have you ever met a French vegetarian?

Negative 8.   A lot of them don't wash. It's a closely guarded secret but that's why they invented perfume.

Negative 9.   They're pathetically old-fashioned. Aeons behind in pop music, infotech and trainers.

Negative 10. Basically they're so French.

Grrrhhhh! I gaze out of the window at a dead flat landscape below us. There's an endless patchwork of empty fields, mile upon mile, dotted with the occasional lost-looking farm attached to a road that seems to lead nowhere. Can there actually be people down there? What on earth do they do all day?

An hour has gone past and I've read my magazine and consumed the apple juice and Kit-Kat that Mum has thoughtfully slipped in my backpack and listened to all of the six CDs I've brought. The plane is starting its descent and the flight attendants are checking that we're all belted up and not endangering our lives by having our tables or seats at the wrong angle. Down below the fields are being replaced by a messy jigsaw of motorways, hypermarkets and car parks filled with tiny toy cars. My tummy does an anxious double-flip as I realise we're arriving. The Poiriers, that is Marie-Christine and Matthilde, are going to be at Charles de Gaulle airport to meet me and I'm desperately trying to remember the phrase that Mum spent ages drumming into my head yesterday:

'Bon-jour. Je-suis-ravie-de-vous-revoir.'

It seems you can't just be pleased to see someone in France. You have to be 'ravie'! As in *ravished*? It is *such* a posey language.

I trail behind an endless stream of people, wondering where the 'kind lady' is – probably so engrossed in her *Daily Telegraph* she's forgotten to get off. I'm led on to a long walkway which is abruptly swallowed up by a tunnel. Typical of the French: they can't design an airport that's plain and straightforward like ours. Theirs has to be a design statement – all globes and tubes snaking into each other like intestines. It's like being digested by some huge monster and spewed out.

At last I'm disgorged through passport control and manage to locate the carousel that has my holdall on it. I follow a load of rowdy guys who look like a rugby team towards the 'Sortie' which is French for Exit. I'm hoping they'll provide some sort of cover for the first impression I'm about to make. Because unlike the other people in the airport, who appear to be normally dressed, I'm wearing my navy-blue tweed school coat. Thank you, Mum. There is no one else, not one single person who is in a full-length navy-blue wool coat. I don't care if, as she warned, it snows or sleets or freezes at Easter – I feel humiliated before I've even got out of the airport.

At the 'Sortie' there is a row of French policemen. They're not like friendly English policemen who've been put on street corners especially to tell you the way. These have guns sprouting from their hips and they're scanning the crowd as if hoping to single out a potential victim to shoot. I have to fight my way through a logjam of Japanese people taking photographs of each other to reach the barrier, where I can just detect someone I recognise. Marie-Christine is in a slim knee-length skirt from which her legs, shiny and perfect, disappear into neat kitten-heel shoes. She's wearing a tiny tight little suede jacket and her smartly cut head of hair is clamped to a mobile phone. Beside her is a girl with impossibly long legs. She has cheekbones you could ski down, dark shiny hair swept into a ponytail, a little zip-up jacket and a scarf wound in this year's latest stylish way around her neck. This can only be Matthilde. Three years have certainly worked their magic on her. She has turned into a picture-perfect Parisienne.

Matthilde has spotted me and is nudging her mother. Marie-Christine has snapped her mobile shut. My coat, with me inside it, makes its way reluctantly towards the barrier.

''Annah, comtooagrandee! Ohminyonne! Donmwaunbizoo,' says Marie-Christine, grabbing me and giving me an enthusiastic mwah-mwah on both cheeks.

'Bon-jour. Je-suis-ravie-d'errm-vous-voir,' I manage to mumble in reply.

'Maydisdonshayreetuparlfrançais!' she replies, clearly impressed.

Matthilde, meanwhile, is looking down on me from her superior height. I can feel her eyes resting uncomfortably on my coat. I feel horribly like a tortoise in a shell — I only wish I could draw my head and limbs in and disappear from sight.

'Bonjour, 'Annah,' she says, leaning down and giving me a rather cooler mwah-mwah.

After the tremendous success of my first sentence, Marie-Christine has assumed my French is fluent. She grabs my bag from me and sets off with it in the direction of the taxis, talking to me non-stop.

'Mayalorsquellinelestaxisputetnoudevondejeunaytoudeswee.'

'Pardon?' I try.

'Dimwashayree. Esqutuafam?' she asks, looking at me searchingly.

I stare back wondering what I've done wrong.

Matthilde comes to the rescue. 'Are you 'ungry?'

'Well yes, a bit.' My eye has been caught by a coffee stall selling long crispy ham baguettes and my mouth is already watering.

'In zat case we will eat on ze way 'ome,' announces Marie-Christine, in English to my relief.

The taxi drove at headlong speed into Paris. The driver kept dodging in and out of lanes as if his life depended on it. Maybe he was hungry too. At last we shot down a slip road, swerved under a bridge and arrived in the city itself.

Somehow I hadn't expected Paris to be so like a picture postcard of Paris. It's all cobbles and shutters and balconies, striped awnings and tables on the pavement. There are long tree-lined streets and everywhere people are dressed in a way that is just that indefinable bit smarter than England. I try to put my finger on what makes it all look so incredibly Parisian and come to the conclusion it's to do with the signs in the street which have oddly French lettering. Typically, all of them seem to have something to do with *food*. My tummy rumbles as I think forlornly of those yummy ham baguettes. Marie-Christine is saying something to the driver and he is swerving to a halt at the roadside. We all spill out and she fumbles in her bag for money to pay him.

I pause on the kerbside and get my first whiff of Paris. It's a curious mixture of cigarette smoke, roasted caramel and drains. I suddenly feel swamped by Frenchness. Paris is so over-the-top. It's above and beside and all around me — all it lacks is a man with an accordion belting out 'La vie en rose'.

But Marie-Christine isn't pausing. Heedless of traffic, she is forcing her way across the street with the two of us in tow. Cars skid to a halt as she dices with death. She throws the drivers a dazzling smile and somehow all three of us make it safely to the far side and arrive at the doors of a restaurant. It's a very smart restaurant. There's a man outside in a big orange rubber apron holding a lethal-looking knife. He's hard at work opening oysters. He's piling them up on a great bank of crushed ice and seaweed along with a lot of other threatening-looking marine life which he's arranged in a pattern like some kind of artwork. Inside the doorway Marie-Christine is greeted like an old friend by a waiter in a smart black suit and we are shown to a table.

I squeeze in beside Matthilde and take in the decor while she and her mother pore over the menu. A trip to a restaurant back home tends to be a big event like a birthday treat, and the places we've been to in Normandy are nowhere near as grand. The walls of this restaurant are covered with gilded mirrors and all the waiters have long white aprons. Marie-Christine is spreading a stiff starched napkin over my lap.

'Thees place is very famous for seafood,' she says. 'You must choose something nice.'

The people at the table next to us have what looks like a triple-decker cake stand piled with some of the evil-looking sea-creatures from the man outside. Displayed on the ice is a range of stuff I've only ever come across on the beach. Surely they can't be eating sea urchins?

'Do they have fish?' I ask, hoping maybe to get off lightly with something like fish and chips. I'm not exactly an adventurous eater and the very sight of a shell or a feeler kind of makes my throat close up in shock.

I'm passed a menu where naturally everything is in French but I spot the word 'sole' which luckily for me is the same in both languages.

In the end Marie-Christine chooses a dozen oysters with a glass of white wine. Matthilde has a plate of huge prawns with a side salad and I have my sole which isn't in batter and doesn't come with chips but with steamed potatoes covered in butter and parsley.

Some time later, as I wipe my bread around the last of the butter, which it seems is an OK thing to do in France, I feel somewhat less apprehensive about French food. Maybe I'm not going to starve to death after all.

Conversation during the meal hasn't been a problem either. Marie-Christine speaks almost perfect English and Matthilde seems to know quite a lot. But this brief interlude of normal communication is short-lived. Having finished her oysters, Marie-Christine puts down her napkin and checks her lipstick in her mirror, saying, 'But, of course, we should speak French to 'Annah. You are here to learn French. No?'

'Well yes, but . . .'

'Uh-uh,' she said, waving a finger at me.

'I mean – oui.'

Chapter Two

The Poiriers' flat is in an area of Paris called Les Invalides. Sounds *really* promising. As we climb out of a taxi, I'm relieved to see the people in the street look as able-bodied as anywhere else in Paris.

Their flat is in one of those typical tall French buildings with lots of fancy stonework and a frill of balconies at every window. We are taken up to the sixth floor in a creaking iron lift with a grille you have to work yourself. Mum had told me that both Marie-Christine and her husband are lawyers, so pretty rich. I hadn't expected their place to be so old-fashioned.

Inside the apartment the place is so stark I wonder if maybe they're redecorating. There are bare wooden floors, a lot of uncomfortable little antique chairs covered in cream linen and a couple of chests of drawers polished to a glossy finish. These seem to be having a style war with the strange modern paintings on the walls.

I followed Marie-Christine as she walked across to the windows and threw open the shutters. From the balcony there was a view over a stretch of grass set out with odd conical trees leading to a very large building with a dome.

'That is where Napoleon is buried,' said Marie-Christine, forgetting for a moment about speaking French. 'You could go and see the tomb.'

Sounded like a load of fun. But I smiled politely and said, 'Oh right – lovely!'

Marie-Christine then suggested I should go and unpack and I discovered the truly dire nature of my situation. The apartment only has two bedrooms, so Matthilde and I have to share. I was going to have to put up with Matthilde's high and mighty down-the-nose expression *twenty-four hours a day*.

It seemed Matthilde wasn't too wild about the idea either. She came and lay on her bed and read a book as I took stuff out of my holdall. She had grudgingly cleared two drawers for me and left a small space on one side of the dressing table. I arranged my hairbrush and make-up bag on the ten-centimetre square allotted to me, resolving to get dressed and undressed well away from her gaze, in the privacy of the bathroom.

I was trying to squeeze all my clothes in the drawers when, at the bottom of the holdall, I came across the new top and jeans I'd been planning to wear to the party. The sight of them brought on another wave of fury at the unfairness of it all. By rights I should be at Jess's house now having a big hair and beauty session, preparing for tomorrow – catching up on all the gossip – probably in fits – Jess has a wicked sense of humour. Instead I was stuck here with Miss Poseur of the Year and the big event on the horizon was a trip to see a *tomb*.

I slammed the drawer shut with more force than absolutely necessary.

'Di-don!' said Matthilde, sitting up crossly on one elbow.

'Sorry.'

Matthilde rolled her eyes and lay back on her pillow.

I sat down on my bed. I'd finished my magazine and didn't have anything to read. Matthilde continued turning the pages of her book, seeming blithely unconscious of the fact that I had nothing to do. I sat there for some minutes wondering how on earth I was going to get through the next two weeks. Nowhere had ever felt so foreign. I might as well be planted on some distant planet and have to live with aliens. That's when I remembered I'd promised Mum I'd call her up to say I'd arrived safely. I clicked open my mobile and selected her number, but when it dialled I got a nasty female French voice saying something unintelligible. I stared at my phone dumbly, realising it had something to do with international codes. No doubt Marie-Christine would know what to dial.

I ventured out into the hallway. I could hear Marie-Christine's voice on the phone coming from somewhere down a corridor. I tracked it down to a tiny office. It was hardly more than a cupboard lined with books.

Marie-Christine was seated in front of a laptop with a diary in her hand, intent on her call. Being used to Mum working, I knew better than to disturb her.

I went and hovered in the kitchen, I could have killed for a cup of tea. I wondered if they would be horribly offended if I made one – which was a bit of a challenge in Marie-Christine's kitchen. It was so ultra-modern it had taken me a minute or two to work out the light switch. There was no sign of a kettle. At home everything was to hand, the kettle was out on the worktop with the box of tea bags beside it, and the biscuit tin – *biscuits*! Here there wasn't anything resembling food in sight. I started furtively to search through the cupboards. Strange, foreign packs came to light, nothing resembling tea bags. I leaned up and reached for a promising-looking tin. This brought a cascade of cans and boxes tumbling down on my head. They fell to the floor with a horrible din and a bag of sugar burst open, spilling its contents everywhere. I froze.

Matthilde appeared in the doorway looking cross.

'Kesketoofay?' she demanded.

'I was trying to make a cup of tea,' I said weakly.

'Kwa?'

'Tea.'

Marie-Christine arrived behind her. 'Keskiesepass?' she asked.

'I was trying to make tea and everything fell out.' I could feel myself going scarlet with embarrassment.

'Omapetite!'

'Sorry, I'll clear it up.' I was shoving packs back into the cupboard as fast as I could, wondering desperately how I could sweep up the sugar.

'No,' said Marie-Christine. 'Matthilde will do it.' She then turned to Matthilde and said something at lightning speed in French, which I could only interpret as: 'Why wasn't she looking after me?' Because with a dark look in my direction, Matthilde fetched a brush and pan from a cupboard and put a saucepan of water to heat on the stove.

Silently, she placed three packs in front of me. They had pictures of flowers and leaves on them, they didn't look anything like tea. But I selected one called 'Verveine' and Matthilde took a bag out and dumped it in a cup. She poured boiling water on and I waited as the water turned faintly green. I took a sip. It tasted exactly how you'd imagine pee would taste. I didn't dare ask for milk or sugar.

I took my 'tea' back to the bedroom where Matthilde had reinstalled herself on the bed complete with book and was once again ignoring me. It was at that point my mobile rang.

I clicked it open. It was Mum.

'You OK?'

I considered the possible replies to this.

a) Yes, apart from having to share a room with a hostile alien.

b) And having to drink pee tea.

c) And missing out on tomorrow's party, which I've been looking forward to *for ever*.

'Yes fine, why?' I snapped.

'You promised you'd call as soon as you got there.'

'We had lunch. Then I didn't know the code.'

'But you're fine?'

'Yes.'

'And you're getting along OK with Matthilde?'

I glanced across at Matthilde. She was still lying flat out on her bed treating me as if I was part of the wallpaper.

'Yes,' I snapped.

'Doesn't sound like it.'

'Well, what do you think?'

'Make an effort.'

'I am.'

'What's their apartment like?'

'Posh.'

'Is that all?'

'Very French.'

'OK, I can see there's no point in talking to you while you're in this mood.'

'I am not in a *mood*, Mum.'

'I'll ring you on Sunday, OK?' Heartlessly she rang off.

I clicked my mobile shut.

Marie-Christine appeared in the doorway and said something incomprehensible to Matthilde. But whatever it was seemed to rouse her and she half-heartedly suggested that we: 'Go see the tom' of Napoleon?'

I shrugged. I wasn't going to give her the satisfaction of leaping to attention. 'If you like.'

'No. Eez if *you* like.'

'You decide.'

Matthilde rolled her eyes and closed her book. Grudgingly, she swung her legs over the side of the bed, raised herself to full height and reached for her jacket. I watched as she stood in front of the mirror, zipping up her jacket and winding her scarf with a professional flourish.

Once she'd finished admiring her reflection, she said, 'OK, we go.' I dragged on my coat and trailed after her. Tomb or no tomb, anything was better than sitting on my bed watching her reading her book.

Actually, as tombs go, Napoleon had one of the better ones. It was totally OTT, like a gi-normous marble sleigh bed on legs. Which explained the dome. Well, you'd have to have something pretty grand to go over a tomb like that. There was a balcony built round on which all these serious silent people stood respectfully looking down at the tomb. Down below there were plaques on the walls commemorating all the victories Napoleon had won in a really showing-off sort of way. Frankly, it made you want to shout 'Trafalgar!' really loudly.

Matthilde showed me round it seeming rather proud of a person I'd always been told was a cruel and ruthless dictator. But I guess if you were on his side, you'd see things differently.

We got back to find that Matthilde's father was home. He opened the door to us and Matthilde made a great fuss of him, calling him 'Papa' in a sickly sweet tone that was positively puke-making. He was tall, balding slightly and wearing a smart grey business suit and the kind of cool designer steel-rimmed glasses you generally see on a younger person. He greeted me oozing fake charm, taking my hand and giving a little half bow over it as if he was going to kiss it or something. But I wasn't going to fall for it. This was precisely what I'd been expecting – typical French behaviour – totally insincere.

'But you are almost as beautifool as your motheur!' he said.

'Merci, monsieur,' I said coolly, in response to this dubious compliment. Christ, I hope not: Mum's well over forty!

Seeing as Matthilde's father was back, it occurred to me that it was getting on for supper time. There was no sign of a meal being prepared. Marie-Christine was still at her desk and I wondered somewhat anxiously whether the lunch we'd had was going to be 'it'. No wonder French people tend to be thinner than us. Back home around this time I'd be changing into my slippers, delving into the fridge, slumping down on the sofa in front of the telly. But it seemed there was going to be no kind of slumming it in this household.

'Not "monsieur", you must call me Pierre,' Matthilde's dad continued. 'And how is your lovely motheur? I remember her well. In Grenoble. We were students together.'

I stared at him, trying to picture a younger, less bald Pierre, long-haired even – probably dressed in a polo neck and jeans, a Gitane no doubt glued between his fingers. And not yet married to Marie-Christine.

I followed him into the living room where he was mixing himself an aperitif. Matthilde had disappeared into our bedroom with her mobile. I was left alone with Pierre to be oozed at. He offered me a drink and when I refused, saying rather primly that I wasn't allowed alcohol, he said, 'But of course not, I was going to mix you something far more special.'

He went into the kitchen and came back with a long glass chinking with ice filled with what looked like orange juice with a splash of something red dissolving in it.

'Orange et grenadine, tchin-tchin,' he said, lifting his glass. 'Come and sit down and tell me all about your motheur.'

'Tchin-tchin,' I said and took a sip. It was quite nice actually.

Why was he so interested in Mum? I eyed him suspiciously. Maybe he'd tried his charm on her. Way back in those student days they'd shared. Maybe he'd even snogged her! This thought made me feel kind of weird.

I told him how Mum was now working as a freelance translator and how she was at a conference in Amsterdam all next week. And I told him about Dad too. In fact, I laid it on a bit about Dad. I suddenly felt rather protective of him. Dad's a history teacher at a not terribly successful comprehensive. It's a nightmare job and he often comes home totally frazzled. But he actually gets some of his students into university, which is a bit of a victory in a school like his.

Pierre then asked me what I thought of our current Prime Minister and I suddenly found I was way out of my depth trying to come up with my own personal views on British politics. But he kept up the fake charm, making a big play of listening to everything I had to say, giving the odd comment here and there, as if my opinions mattered.

By this time Marie-Christine had emerged from her office and promising sounds and smells had started to waft through from the kitchen. Matthilde appeared with a tablecloth and a pile of knives and forks and gave me one of her looks, which I interpreted as an invitation to help her. So I escaped from Pierre before I could display too much ignorance, to lay the table.

Dinner at the Poiriers' was a far cry from Mum's familiar spag bol and casseroles. We started with some strange little dishes shaped like the Shell symbol, filled with hot seafood in a creamy sauce which Marie-Christine said apologetically had come from someone who sounded extremely untrustworthy called a 'traitor'. I did my best to force mine down with a lot of bread and hid the wibbly bit under my shell – it was bright orange and tasted of car tyres. Pierre insisted I had the tiniest sip of white wine in my glass as it was a special bottle from somewhere called 'Alsace' and very light.

I noticed that both Matthilde and Marie-Christine fussed around Pierre as if he were royalty. There was none of the free-for-all we had at home. It seemed Pierre's only task was to look after the wine: to open it, to taste it and to pour it. After the first course, which they called the 'entrée', we had 'bifstek' and salad. The steaks looked lovely and brown on the outside but when you cut into them they were so raw they were all blood and jelly. I did my best to eat all the outside with loads more bread. I felt pretty full after all that bread but afterwards there was a huge plate of cheese and a yummy apple tart. So all in all I went to bed that night feeling totally stuffed.

I hoped to be asleep by the time Matthilde joined me. No such luck. Just as I was dropping off, she barged into the room. She spent ages at the dressing table doing stuff with cotton wool and cleansing lotion although as far as I could see she didn't wear a speck of make-up. After that she had a long whispered conversation under the covers on her mobile then she reached for her book. I was really tired but I can never sleep with the light on. Whatever she was reading held her attention for a good half hour. Knowing the French it was probably something incredibly intellectual like Mum is always going on about, like Jean-Paul Sartre or Colette.

I passed the time going through a mental checklist of positives and negatives about my first day in France.

Negatives:

1)   Posiness – all this fuss about table napkins and wine tasting.

2)   Boringness – tomb visiting was the high point of the day.

3)   Smells – Paris has smells which could keep Dyno-Rod at work round the clock.

Positives – I could only think of one:

1)   French bread.

The following morning I woke to find Matthilde was already up and in the shower. My watch told me it was eight o'clock but it felt horribly early because of the time difference. I hauled myself out of bed to find Marie-Christine bustling in and out of her bedroom with piles of shirts. She was packing a suitcase for Pierre. Pierre was fussing back and forth with his mobile, muttering something about a taxi and Charles de Gaulle.

When I enquired where he was going, he said he was off to New York for three weeks so would not see me again before I left. He hoped I'd have a great time with Matthilde. I replied, with as much conviction as I could summon, that I was sure I would.

At last his taxi arrived and he and Marie-Christine went into a long and passionate exchange of goodbyes. Matthilde came out of the bathroom and joined in. The way they were behaving you'd think he was off to a *war*. French people are so over-the-top. Having shaken himself free, Pierre kissed me too and told me to 'be good'. Fat chance of being anything else in the circumstances.

Once Pierre had left, Marie-Christine and Matthilde started a long conversation in the hallway in which I couldn't help noticing my name occurred frequently. It was 'Annah this and 'Annah that and they were both raising their voices. Marie-Christine finished by saying: 'Aytootoccoop d'Annahtootlajournay. Jaydootraveye!'

Matthilde flounced into the bedroom, giving me the blackest of her dark looks. She slumped down on the bed and plugged herself into her iPod and turned the volume up. I could hear its irritating tinkle from my side of the room. Extra irritating because I didn't actually have an iPod. I was saving up for one. Dad said if I could pay half, he'd pay the other. No doubt Matthilde's was simply doled out to her by her oh-so-loving father.

Marie-Christine popped her head round the door, took one look at Matthilde and turned to me: 'Chérie – do you like croissants for your breakfast?'

'Ummm. Oh yes please.'

I joined her in the hallway, she was holding out a twenty-euro note. 'You like to go to the boulangerie for me?'

Why not? Since the alternative was passive iPod listening. I nodded and took the note while Marie-Christine gave me instructions.

She wanted a baguette, three croissants, two pains chocolats and anything else I thought looked nice. She wrote down the 'digi-code' for me which was a number I had to tap into a box to get back into the building.

'You think you will be OK?'

'Oui.'

Come on, I'm nearly fourteen for godsake, buying bread isn't exactly rocket science.

I went down nonchalantly in the lift. The bread shop was a couple of blocks down. You couldn't miss it, it had BOULANGERIE in big thick scrolly gold letters over the window and when I opened the door a delicious smell of freshly baked bread wafted out to greet me.

I asked in my best French: 'Trois croissants, deux pains chocolats, une baguette et . . .'

My eye had been caught by a raspberry tart. It was red and glossy and packed with huge ripe raspberries and you could just see the teeniest glimpse of the custard cream underneath. I could feel my mouth watering.

The boulangerie lady was looking at me with grave disapproval.

'Bonjour, mademoiselle.'

'Bonjour,' I replied, remembering too late that it's horribly rude in France not to greet people in shops before ordering. I tried the list on her again.

This time she grumpily shoved the croissants and pains chocolats in a bag. She reached down a baguette and rolled it in white paper.

'Ay-avec-sa?'

'Errrrm?'

'Say-too?'

My eye returned to the raspberry tart.

She followed my gaze and lifted out the tart. Before I could stop her she'd packed it in a smart gold box and tied it with a bow and, taking a ribbon, she ran it over with her scissors to give it curly ends and plonked a gold sticker on it. Well, Marie-Christine did say anything else I liked the look of, didn't she?

I handed over the twenty-euro note and got a few very small coins back. I realised sinkingly that the tart must have been horribly expensive. I wondered if I should try to get the lady to take it back, but this was way beyond my French and she had taken an awful lot of trouble packing it. Besides, she was still looking cross. So I said, 'Merci' and hurriedly left the shop.

I made my way back carrying my very expensive purchase in its beautiful gold box. I now noticed there were plane trees all the way down the street that were just coming into leaf. They had wonderful dappled bark, kind of like camouflage, and each one was growing out of a fancy ironwork grille. I noticed the people too. The sun was coming out and they were walking in a happy kind of way, hand in hand or with dogs or prams, and quite a few of them were carrying baguettes like me. They were holding them up as if they were some kind of emblem or symbol of Frenchness.

I liked this idea and I was just working out how I was going to write it down on a postcard to send to Dad, maybe with a drawing too, when I realised that I must have missed the Poiriers' building. Not difficult to do, because all the buildings in the street looked exactly alike. They even had the same big shiny black doors.

I paused and looked back down the street. I could no longer see the boulangerie, so I started tracking my way back and, as I did so, I had the horrible realisation that I had no idea what number the Poiriers lived at. None of the doors had names beside them, they all had anonymous brass digi-boxes just like the Poiriers. And I didn't have my mobile on me. I could picture it now, lying on the bedside table in Matthilde's room.

I start walking faster. Surely there must be something I remember? Was their building before or after that café? There are several cafés and they all look alike. The trees look alike too. I turn back again and stare up at the row of identical buildings. All of them have precisely the same long windows and black iron balconies. I scan the people in the street, wondering if any of them might know the Poiriers. My heart is thumping in my chest now and my hands have gone sweaty. This is such a stupid situation.

I go down the street and find the boulangerie again and then slowly make my way back, examining each house in turn for something familiar. But it's no use, it could be any one of them. So I slump down on a bench to think the thing through. I'm really hungry now and that doesn't help. The most wonderful vanilla-and-caramel aroma is coming from the bag of croissants and they're still warm. I take the teensiest nibble at one. Which leads to a bite. Then suddenly I'm one croissant down. But my brain is starting to function. I could go to a police station. But French policemen don't look nice and friendly like English policemen. I could go to every door and try the number Marie-Christine gave me in each digi-box. But I'd look really suspicious doing that – like a burglar.

Maybe a better idea would be to ask in a café. According to Mum, Parisian people spend half their lives in their local café, someone would be bound to know them. I select the café that looks the most welcoming and make for it. I'm peering through the glass trying to decide if the people inside look friendly or not when I'm stopped short.

Surely not. It can't be? There's a woman who looks exactly like Marie-Christine seated at a table with her back to me. She's sitting opposite a man, talking to him earnestly. I can see her face reflected in the mirrored wall — it *is* Marie-Christine! I'm flooded with relief and I'm about to bound in and run up to her, when I pause. She's leaning forward and she's grabbed both this man's hands in hers and she's staring into his eyes. I take a step back. This clearly is a very private moment. And that man is not Pierre! I'm shocked to the core. Her husband left a mere half hour ago and there she is, blatantly out with another man. This confirms everything I've suspected about the French.

What do I do now? I back further off and hover behind a tree. I wonder if Matthilde knows about this. Matthilde who is so attached to her dear papa. This is dreadful! Marie-Christine doesn't seem like that kind of person at all. Surely I must be mistaken. I peer round the tree and try to work out what's going on. It's like watching a movie with the sound turned off. The man in front of Marie-Christine is dark and has a shadow of beard as if he hasn't shaved and he's really handsome. He's much handsomer than Pierre, actually. He's leaning forward and shaking his head and now he's bowed it *despairingly* in his hands. I can see Marie-Christine in the mirror again and she's saying something. I try to lip-read. A tough challenge, since I can't understand much French even when I hear it. But I can see Marie-Christine is trying to tell him something really important. She's leaning closer still. Maybe she's doing the right thing, telling him it can never be – or that it's all over. I can feel tears of sympathy pricking in my eyes . . .

''Annah!' a voice exclaims behind me. I nearly jump out of my skin. It's Matthilde. She's standing staring at me as if I'm the dumbest person in the whole world. Oh-my-god – whatever happens she mustn't see her mother!

'Hi. I got lost.'

'Kwa?'

'La maison. Je non know le numéro.'

'Perdue?' asks Matthilde.

It's a word I recognise. It's in the title of some book Mum goes on and on about.

'Oui,' I say weakly.

Matthilde does *the* most over-the-top eye-roll and shrug and to my intense relief turns on her heel. She sets off in the opposite direction from the café. The way she is walking demonstrates exactly how she feels about me. I follow behind like some lost dog – totally humiliated. Geesus, what a morning – and I haven't even had proper breakfast yet.

Inside the apartment the table is laid with three bowls, three spoons and a pot of jam. Matthilde ignores me and sets about heating milk in the kitchen. I put the bread and bag of croissants on the table and wonder what to do with the raspberry tart. I simply can't face Matthilde's scorn when I explain that I didn't mean to buy it, it was a terrible mistake. So I go very quietly to the bedroom and hide it under my bed.

When I come back, Matthilde carries in two bowls of frothy hot chocolate. She seats herself at the table and, with a nod in the direction of her mother's bowl, she says, 'Maman 'as gone out.'

I nod, trying to look as if I didn't know.

The hot chocolate is yummy and I copy Matthilde as she dips a croissant in it and kind of slurps. It seems things like dunking and slurping and plate wiping are perfectly all right in France. I have grudgingly to admit this is a small but significant bonus.

We've finished breakfast and there's still no sign of Marie-Christine. My brain is busy inventing dramatic scenarios. She's going to appear in the doorway at any moment, pale and tearful, and announce that she is packing her bags and leaving with her mystery lover *for ever*. Or maybe she's dumped him and he's suicidal – he's threatening to throw them both in the Seine or maybe off the Eiffel Tower. Or even worse, he's taken out a gun and is about to shoot the two of them, in fact right now he's spraying the café with bullets! In each of these cases I wonder what will happen to Matthilde and me once we're left alone together. Will the police have to break into the apartment to find our decomposing remains because we've *throttled each other*?

I watch Matthilde as she calmly takes the hot chocolate bowls and loads them in the dishwasher. She seems totally unaware of the impending disaster that is about to descend on her.

Having finished tidying up the breakfast, Matthilde returns to her natural habitat – bed, book and iPod. I pick up a newspaper that has been left on the table and follow her. I settle down on my bed and try to make some sort of sense out of the headlines. Failing this I resort to looking at the pictures. The usual selection of violence, death and terror does nothing to make me feel better. Still no sign of Marie-Christine.

Suddenly Matthilde sits bolt upright, takes her earphones out of her ears and says, 'I sink we go shopping.'

'Shopping?'

She nods. Shopping. The very normality of this brings me back to my senses. It seems French girls may be human after all. Whatever has happened to Marie-Christine, Matthilde doesn't seem concerned. There's probably a totally innocent explanation.

Chapter Three

We didn't go to a shop, we went to a market. I'd been looking forward to checking out the latest fashions — after all I was in Paris. But no, this market — in its typically French obsessional way — sells nothing but food. It's in a street called the Rue Cler and as we turn into it I'm stopped in my tracks.

'Look!' I say to Matthilde.

'Kwa?'

It was the Eiffel Tower! We had a view of it full on, down a side street. It was really close, literally towering over the buildings.

Matthilde shrugged as if she saw it every day. Which she probably did, I suppose. 'Oh oui, la Tour Eiffel.'

'Can't we go up?'

'Go up?'

'Errm, monter?'

Big mistake. This was of course the naffest of uncool things to suggest.

'La Tour Eiffel eez for tourists,' Matthilde said dismissively.

I stood my ground. 'But I *am* a tourist.'

'Per'aps,' she said and turned her attention to a fruit and vegetable stall. I gaze miserably at the carefully stacked pyramids of produce. By rights I should be down the mall right now. Doing a last-minute clothing check with Jess, maybe finding the ultimate accessory for the party. Instead, I'm faced with a riveting choice of vegetables.

It's not long before I discover the real reason I've been taken to the market. I'm the beast of burden. Matthilde shops with the dedication of a proper grown-up French woman, squeezing things and demanding to have a taste before she buys, while I tag along behind, having bags loaded on me. Soon I'm weighed down with a knobbly bag of artichokes, a couple of kilos of oranges, some tiny long potatoes, broccoli, some stringy-looking salad, celery the size of a small tree, a cabbage, a kilo of red onions and some extremely smelly cheese.

On the way back to the apartment, even though Matthilde has kindly taken one or two of the lighter packages, I feel as if my arms are being stretched to way below my knees. We pass the café where earlier I'd seen Marie-Christine with her mystery man. I scan through the window. The table they were sitting at is now deserted. But the memory of that moment comes back to me with full force. The way she was leaning forward, how he bowed his head in his hands . . . Something really serious was going on, I know it was.

Matthilde is opening the front door, calling out a bright 'Coo-coo, Maman!'

She pauses in the hallway and puts down the shopping. 'Maman?'

She pushes open Marie-Christine's bedroom door. A small suitcase is lying on the bed, a few clothes already inside it. She's packing! My heart does a double somersault as all my suspicions come back sevenfold.

'Maman?' says Matthilde, tracking her way down the corridor to where a quiet and hurried voice can be heard coming from Marie-Christine's study.

Matthilde throws open the door and leans on the doorframe.

'Mamanjayfaylaycorse.'

But Marie-Christine is holding up a hand to her, listening intently to whoever it is at the other end of the phone.

'Oui d'akkor. Ase-swar,' she finishes and puts down the phone.

She gets up from her desk and there is a rapid exchange between her and Matthilde. Whatever she is saying doesn't please Matthilde one bit.

There is a lot of 'May-non, Maman!' And I think I can even discern the fact that Matthilde was actually intending to take me up the Eiffel Tower. But this could be mere invention on my part.

Then Marie-Christine turns to me. ''Annah, chérie. I'm afraid I 'ave some ve-ry important work. I 'ave to take you to the country. To my mother — Matthilde's grandparents' 'ouse. Is nice there. You will like.'

Very important work, indeed! I am so shocked, I'm lost for words. Marie-Christine is most definitely up to something with her dark and handsome stranger. So we're being sent to the country. I stare at her as the full significance of this sinks in. The country — at Easter — with Matthilde. I will like? NOT!

I can hear Matthilde opening and closing her wardrobe and I join her to find she is furiously dumping stuff in a suitcase. I do likewise, in a kind of action rewind of yesterday's unpacking. I've no idea where we're going. But if it's anything like Normandy in April, it'll be a load of damp fields lost in mist where *even the cows look depressed*. For a moment the shared activity of packing feels vaguely bonding. Matthilde raises an eyebrow at me and says in a furious undertone, 'Maman! Typique!'

I nod in agreement as we lug our stuff into the hallway where Marie-Christine is already waiting with a pile of bags beside her and her car keys in her hand. It takes ages to get out of the apartment because every door has to be locked and the alarm put on and then Matthilde suddenly remembers the stuff we just bought in the market and we have to unlock everything to go back in. We go down in hostile silence in the lift. At the bottom Matthilde gives all our shopping to a lady who lives on the ground floor who's called the 'concierge'.

We then go down one more floor to an underground car park and we are just about to get in Marie-Christine's car when Matthilde exclaims, 'Zoot, nouzavons oublié Edith!'

Now 'oublié' is a word I recognise. It means 'forgot'. I know because of the word 'oubliette' which is a really horrible sort of hole you leave people in to torture them. I learnt about it in history, although I can't remember when it was, or who did it to whom, but the gruesome bit kind of stuck.

'Edith?' queries Marie-Christine.

'Edith Piaf!' says Matthilde. She and her mother then go into a long argument in which the word 'concierge' comes up several times.

Edith Piaf I do know about. She's a really famous French singer who there's been a film about. But I thought Edith Piaf was dead.

It seems that Matthilde has won the argument. Marie-Christine leaves the car with a sigh and we all have to troop back upstairs and unlock the apartment and turn off the burglar alarm and go through the kitchen and unlock the back door and go out on to a kind of fire escape where there is a cage with Edith in it. Edith is small and really fluffy and she doesn't look at all grateful for being remembered. In fact, she scrabbles in her wood shavings and buries herself.

'Oh, a guinea pig!' I say.

'Un cochon d'Inde,' Matthilde corrects me.

So at last we leave Paris. Matthilde, of course, is in the front seat beside Marie-Christine because she has the longer legs. I'm squashed in the back with Edith in her cage. We haven't gone very far before I realise why Edith spends her life on the fire escape. Like their larger relatives, guinea pigs are horribly smelly. I'm starting to feel sick before we've got to the top of the street.

This isn't helped by the way Marie-Christine drives. I noticed when she climbed into the car that she was wearing really high heels and I wonder whether this might be the cause of it – maybe her toe can't reach the brake pedal. She is also putting on lipstick as she drives, she's swung the rear-view mirror round so she can see what she's doing, which I know for a fact is totally illegal. And what's more, we're coming up to a junction where cars seem to be entering from all angles. There is an island with a massive archway in the middle which has a load of horses and stuff on top and all the drivers are hurtling towards it, trying to be the first to get round. Marie-Christine has snapped her lipstick shut and is sending dazzling smiles to the other drivers while barging out in front as if she owns the place. She circumnavigates the archway with the skill of a Formula One driver.

Glancing over her shoulder at me, she says blithely, 'No right of way at Etoile. You just 'ave to go for it!'

'Oh yes, right,' I gulp as she narrowly misses a car coming in from our right.

I don't want to go into the details of that drive. Only to say that it took around three hours. That I wasn't actually sick but perhaps I would have felt better if I had been. Towards the end of the third hour I was allowed to have the window down and I started to feel better.

In fact, I began to feel quite hungry. Which is when I remembered the raspberry tart. The thought of it, abandoned under the bed inside its beautiful gold box, really got to me.

I sat miserably in the back of the car, imagining the tart decomposing. Its wonderful translucent glaze would be the first thing to go. Gradually it would turn opaque and a mist of grey fluffy bacteria would grow over the surface. Inside it would turn to jelly, cracking and fissuring as the raspberries slowly dissolved, disintegrating into pulp and leaving a floating plankton of pips. Finally a thick white penicillin-type mould would surge up from the custard-cream layer, a bit like a volcano erupting. Then the whole lot would gradually soak through the box. At some point it would stick hard to the floor.

Hopefully, I'd be safely back in England by the time the Poiriers discovered it.

During the drive I had time to modify my French checklist somewhat.

I add:

Negatives:

1) French driving — their logic seems to be: as long as you're far enough in front no one can crash into you.

2) French countryside — I think the kilometres must be longer in France or something — it goes on for ever.

Positives:

1) Feeling too sick to think of any.

At last we arrived at a couple of massive gateposts which were carved with the words 'Les Rochers'. Marie-Christine swerved off the main road. I roused myself and stared out of the window. The car crunched down a long gravel drive between an avenue of trees, gnarled into weird knobby shapes. And then I got my first sighting of the 'house'. Oh-my-god!

I remembered something Mum had said about Marie-Christine's father being 'rather grand'; he had a title of some kind, according to Mum. Dad had scoffed at this, saying all that kind of thing had been done away with during the French Revolution. But judging by the building up ahead, a few stones had been left unturned.

This wasn't just a 'house', it was a château. In fact, it might well have been the model for all those Walt Disney imitations. It was a crumbling stone building with four towers topped by witch's-hat roofs. Huge cedar trees on either side gave it a dark and brooding appearance. And some kind of vine or creeper had spread in an evil way, covering some of the windows. It was the kind of place the word 'spooky' had been invented to describe.

The baying of two vicious-looking black dogs completed the impression. They bounded out towards the car, leaping at it as if they were going to tear our throats out the minute we opened the doors. The car came to a halt and Marie-Christine turned to me and said, 'Mais voilà. We 'ave arrived.'

I crouched in the back with Edith Piaf, watching in horror as with cries of 'Sultan!', 'Titan' Matthilde opened her door and threw her arms around the first dog. The other joined in and there was a great display of doggy affection.

A tall severe-looking lady, with hair swept back into a bun, emerged from the house. Marie-Christine climbed out of the car and went to greet her. After a lot of kissing, Marie-Christine introduced me to the lady.

''Annah, je présente Madame de Lafitte, ma mère.'

The lady leaned down to kiss me too, only it wasn't really a kiss. It was the faintest touching of cheeks on either side. Her cheeks were very soft and smelt of some sort of soap, fresh and lemony.

I followed them into a dimly lit hallway which was big enough to fit our whole house in. It had a stone flagged floor, a massive oak staircase and simply miles above us there was a beamed ceiling. The walls were hung with tapestries and dotted around were the decapitated heads of various animals – a couple of stags, something that looked like a moose and a ferocious wild boar whose glass eyes glinted angrily as they caught the light. I shivered. Inside the house it was icy cold.

Matthilde had been told to show me to my room and I trailed behind her up the stairs as Marie-Christine and her mother disappeared into a side room deep in conversation. The door closed behind them with a dull echo. Once upstairs, Matthilde led me down a corridor flanked by doors. She threw one open.

'You sleep 'ere,' she said. I walked in. It was a huge high room with a four-poster bed with curtains round it. The walls were of an odd dark red colour and the furniture was heavy old-fashioned stuff. There was a huge fireplace with an ancient blotchy mirror above it. But there wasn't a fire, or a radiator, or any other kind of heating as far as I could see.

I turned to find Matthilde had left me there. It seemed we didn't have to share. My heart sank; in a house like this sharing would have been rather reassuring, even if it had to be with Matthilde. I went over to the bed and pulled back the heavy curtains. It was the kind of bed that made you wonder if someone had died in it. Which I realised was highly probable since it looked incredibly old. I dumped my holdall on a marble-topped chest of drawers. The room had various doors leading off into cobwebby cupboards; no sign of a bathroom, which I could do with actually, after that drive.

'Matthilde?' I called down the corridor. My voice echoed eerily in the emptiness. There was no answer. I went to the stairwell and called her name again. Still no answer. So I tried each door in turn. These opened on to more bedrooms, equally cold with similarly grand beds but obviously not used — the furniture was draped with eerie-looking dustsheets. In the end I found a bathroom. Inside, everything was antique too. There was a huge stained bath on legs, a giant's washbasin and a loo with a wonky seat. It had an old-fashioned cistern with a chain you had to pull. The taps coughed and spluttered and reluctantly supplied me with a trickle of icy water. It didn't look as if anything had changed since the house had been built.

I called Matthilde again. Still no response. So I made my way back to my room and stared out of the window. It had been grey overcast weather all the way down from Paris. Now rain threatened. I looked out over the drive-way and down that avenue. There seemed to be a moat at the end crossed by a stone bridge. We must have driven over it. On either side of the avenue, there were lawns of lumpy grass. Beyond these there was bleak open countryside which faded away into damp grey mist.

I could hear footsteps on the gravel below and leaning forward I caught sight of Marie-Christine returning to her car. I watched as Madame de Lafitte followed, talking urgently. She seemed upset about something. Matthilde came into view and hovered at a distance. Then Marie-Christine kissed them both and drove off without a backward glance.

I watched the car disappearing from sight. Was Marie-Christine going off for a secret rendezvous with her dark and handsome stranger? Why was everyone so upset? But whatever she was up to, it seemed I had been left here, with a snooty French girl and a strict old lady in a house that was huge, cold and, worst of all, probably *haunted*! The sound of the car wheels crunching on the gravel grew fainter and fainter and then faded away into silence. I stood staring out of the window. There was no wind in the trees. Nothing moved in the garden. The house was eerily still.

I slumped down on the bed and, reaching for my mobile, I dialled up Mum. A good moan at her might make me feel better. But her phone was on answerphone. Then I dialled up Jess. She wasn't answering either which made me feel really down. I left her a text:

abandoned in
haunted house
eeeeek!
me x

I sat on the bed for quite a long time after that, wondering why Jess wasn't answering. And then I realised that everyone would be round at Angie's right now, having a girly time getting ready for the party. Her mobile was probably buried under a load of coats. Or maybe they had the music on really loud and she couldn't hear the ringtone. At any rate, she was clearly too busy enjoying herself to bother about me.

At that thought I felt *really* sorry for myself. I went back to the window. Darkness was closing in. Grey fingers of mist were drifting in across the lawn. The avenue of trees stood out against it like a row of spooky figures, their knobbly branches reaching down as if they were waiting to trap you if you tried to escape.

Abruptly the silence was broken. Something had startled some evil black birds; they flew up angrily circling the far end of the park, their hoarse cries echoing harshly in the stillness. One of the dogs bayed somewhere down below. I shivered. If this was in a film, it would never've got passed for PG.

I turned my back on the window. The furniture looked dark and lumpy in the twilight. Fleetingly it reminded me of something. The red room! The room Jane Eyre had been locked in by her horrid stepmother. When we'd read it at school, I'd thought that Jane was making a childish fuss over nothing. But now I knew just how she felt. I went to the light switch and turned the light on. There was a single central light with a heavy fringed shade; it lit the room dimly, making the furniture cast long shadows. How was I ever going to sleep here *alone*?

My door was flung open at that point.

'Poorkwatoonedescend?'

'What?'

'Grandmère ask why you no come down?'

'Oh, I didn't know I was meant to.'

Matthilde shrugged in non-comprehension and swept out of the room, so I followed her. She led me down the stairwell and across the hallway to a great oak door which opened with a traditional ghost-story creak on to a large dining room.

'Voici!' called out Matthilde.

I paused, taking in the room. The ceiling had huge oak beams like an old English Tudor house and the floor was made of great slabs of stone. There was a stone fireplace big enough to sit in with a coat of arms carved in the centre. A fire of giant logs was burning in it. The dogs were stretched out in front of the fire as if trying to soak in its warmth before it escaped into the room. A long oak table was laid for four people. I was just wondering who the fourth could be when I heard an unnerving kind of tapping and dragging noise coming from the hallway. The door slid open and an old gentleman came into the room. He was short with bright white hair and a moustache. He was walking carefully with a stick. He looked far too old to be married to Madame de Lafitte.

'Ahmondiuh!' he said, catching sight of me and stopping in his tracks. 'Caroline!'

'No,' I said, shaking my head as he lurched forward to

greet me. With sudden inspiration I came out with one of my few reliable French phrases: 'Je m'appelle Hannah.'

'Maynon,' he said, looking confused and staring at me hard. 'Comtooresemble Caroline!'

'I'm Hannah,' I said. 'I've just arrived from England.'

He smiled sadly. 'It is a long time since I hear English, Caroline.'

I was surprised to hear that he spoke English so well, and oddly with an American accent. He signalled to the table and shuffled towards it. I followed as he sank with a sigh into his chair.

At that point Matthilde's grandmother came in. She was carrying a heavy white tureen with a checked cloth wrapped around it.

'MayGeraldine, toonarianditdelarrivaydeCaroline?' I heard him say.

Madame de Lafitte placed the tureen on the table and sat down saying, 'Maynon, Charles. Senaypas Caroline. Elle s'appelle 'Annah. A table, mes petites.'

Then she turned to me. ''Annah, jeteprésente Oncle Charles.'

'Bonjour, monsieur,' I said as I took my seat.

'Bonsoir, Oncle Charles,' said Matthilde and went up and kissed him on both cheeks.

I wondered who he was confusing me with. And also why he spoke English with that accent. It was all very strange. Madame de Lafitte took out the old man's napkin and shook it then tucked it into his collar. Then she ladled soup into shallow dishes and Matthilde passed them round. It was a strange thin soup that had strands of some vegetable in it that I didn't recognise but it was hot and warming. The old man slurped every spoonful, he had two bowls full.

It was a rather uncomfortable meal. Matthilde's grand-mother sat on the edge of her seat with a poker-straight back. She seemed lost in thought and served us with a distracted air. I noticed that Matthilde answered her only when she was spoken to and in a really polite fashion. As we ate, the only sound, apart from the solemn ticking of a tall clock in the corner, came from old Oncle Charles. We had boiled fish after the soup with a lumpy sauce and mashed potatoes. Then Madame de Lafitte brought out a bowl of funny white cheese that tasted like yogurt. It wasn't too bad with sugar on it.

As I ate, my mind kept returning to Angie's party. Angie's dad had cleaned out their double garage for it. He'd hired some disco lights and said he'd do something about the funny car smell. People would be arriving right now. Mark wouldn't be there yet. He probably wouldn't turn up till quite late. He'd notice I wasn't there, of course. He'd ask where I was and Angie would say, 'Oh she's in Paris,' as she'd been primed to, hopefully making it sound really cool and grown-up. And he'd be intrigued, picturing me in some smart Parisian café surrounded by drop-dead-gorgeous people. Instead of me sitting here in the middle of nowhere with Matthilde and her strict grandmother, eating boiled fish and mashed potato with an old man who thought I was someone else and was obviously completely dotty!

After dinner old Oncle Charles got up wearily.

He said 'Bonne nuit' to everyone and then he turned to me.

'So long, Caroline. Maybe we can chew the fat tomorrow.'

'Yes,' I said, wondering what this weird expression meant. 'That would be nice.'

To complete the perfect evening, it seemed Matthilde and I were expected to clear away. You'd think a house like theirs would have had loads of servants. And it probably did once. But clearly the de Lafittes had seen better days. When you looked at things closely, you could see how shabby they were. The tapestries were all moth-eaten and the rugs all threadbare and most of the furniture was worn right down to the stuffing.

Matthilde and I had to wash up in this huge kitchen. Needless to say they didn't have a dishwasher. The kitchen didn't have units or worktops or anything, just open shelves and a long scrubbed wooden table down the centre. There was a fireplace with a heavy semicircular iron door which Matthilde said was an old bread oven but they didn't use it any more. And there was a stove that looked like it dated back to before the Second World War.

We washed up in a big chipped sink and stacked the plates in a wooden rack. Matthilde left me to wash, while she faffed around drying and stacking things in a haphazard fashion.

'Who does your uncle think I am?' I asked her. 'Who is this person Caroline?'

She shrugged. ''Eez like that. Eez because 'eez very old.'

The dishes and the tureen we'd had the soup in had to be put away in a back kitchen in a huge oak cupboard with carved doors. Matthilde showed me where the cheese was kept in an icy pantry down a flight of stone steps. It was lined with shelves stacked with bottled fruit and pots of home-made jam and it had a strange smell all of its own, a mixture of damp and wine and cheese and pickles.

While in there I was struck by the idea that — apart from the fact that both of us were dressed in jeans and stuff — we might well have slipped into a time warp and I'd wake up next day and find it was, like, *hundreds of years ago*. And I'd be trapped here working like some skivvy in the kitchen *for ever*. I decided to write this idea down for Dad too and give him a description of the pantry and the bread oven because that was the kind of detailed stuff he liked. Then I remembered that I hadn't even had time to buy postcards in Paris.

Matthilde didn't seem to have anything planned for after dinner – *surprise, surprise*. Her grandmother went off to her room and Matthilde settled herself down with a book in the only comfortable chair beside the fire. It had got even colder and I could hear rain beating against the windowpane. Having managed to communicate the fact that I needed paper and an envelope, I chose the warmer side of the table to tackle the ancient craft of letter writing.

I sat there trying to work out a suitable way to tell Dad about my dire situation, without being too much of a pain. Writing anything was daunting as Madame de Lafitte had the most valuable-looking notepaper. The envelope was lined with pale grey tissue. The paper was cream and textured and had a crest like the one above the fireplace. It was so thick you could've made lampshades out of it. What could I possibly write which would be grand enough for this paper?

'Dear Dad,' I started. This looked wrong. This was the kind of paper you should start with 'Dear Father' or even 'Dearest Papa'.

By the time I'd finished, I'd used three sheets of paper. When folded, it was hard to get them into the envelope.

Matthilde got up and stretched and announced that she was going 'au lit' so there was nothing for it but to go too. This was the moment I'd been dreading.

With a sinking heart, I followed her up the big oak

staircase, under the dismal gaze of those decapitated animals. Our figures cast long shadows on the walls and I suddenly thought of the hundreds of people who had walked up the staircase before us. Not the best thing to dwell on at this time of night, since all of those people must have died long ago. It made the idea of ghosts seem very real indeed.

When she came to my door, Matthilde turned to me and said, 'Bonne nuit, 'Annah,' giving me the coolest lightest possible mwah-mwah on each cheek before she disappeared round the bend in the corridor.

I steeled myself to go into my bedroom, turning on the light before Matthilde was out of earshot. Matthilde's footsteps continued down the corridor. I heard a door close behind her. Then there was silence.

Nothing had changed in my room. It was as red and dark and spooky as ever. I realised I would have to brave the corridor alone to go to the bathroom. But first, I tried Mum again.

She answered for once.

'You all right, poppet?'

'I s'pose so.'

'What's that meant to mean?'

'I'm not even in Paris. We've been sent to the country. To Matthilde's grandparents'.'

'But why?'

I hesitated, and thought better of telling Mum my suspicions about Marie-Christine.

'Dunno. Marie-Christine had to go off somewhere.'

'Are you at Les Rochers?'

'Yes – it's miles from anywhere.'

'That house! It dates back to the thirteenth century!'

'I know, it's practically falling down.'

'But how wonderful!'

'Wonderful! It's icy cold. All the way from Paris I was in the back of the car with a smelly guinea pig. I was nearly sick. Nothing works here – they don't even have a dishwasher.'

'Oh, poor baby.'

'Well, it's not fair. I didn't even get to go up the Eiffel Tower.'

'How's your French coming on?' said Mum, diplomatically changing the subject.

But I wasn't having it. '. . . and there's an old man here, who's some sort of ancient uncle of Matthilde's. He thinks I'm someone else and he slurps his soup. Can't I come home?'

'You mean old Monsieur de Lafitte is still alive?'

'Only just. He's totally dotty. Mum, I'm missing tons of things back home, it's not fair.'

'You can't possibly leave now. The Poiriers would be really hurt.'

'But there's nothing to do here. It's raining. It's horrid.'

'Are you getting on any better with Matthilde?'

'What do you think?'

'Well, it's probably quite difficult for her too. Not speaking the same language. You have to try and see it from her point of view.'

'I knew you'd be on her side.'

'I'm not on anyone's side.'

'I bet Dad would let me come home.'

'Your father's got enough on his plate. He's got assessments, coursework, exams to mark. You're not to bother him.'

I thought back to Dad, the night before I'd left. He had looked pretty frayed.

'Look, Hannah. This is a real opportunity for you to learn French. Honestly, darling, it's not as if you're in a war zone.'

'But, Mum, this house is really spooky. It could be haunted.'

'Haunted? Is this what it's all about?' She was laughing at me now. I could hear her. 'There are no such things as ghosts. You know there aren't.'

'That doesn't stop it being spooky.'

'Oh, Hannah, come on, grow up.'

'I knew you wouldn't understand.'

'Look, I've got to go now. Chin up, OK?'

'But, Mum . . .' She'd rung off. How could a mother be so unfeeling! I bet she wouldn't like it here. Not in a war zone! Huh! At least war zones were generally in places that were warm, and had people in them and saw some action from time to time! Not miserably cold and dark and where you had to brave at least twenty metres of haunted corridor to get to the most basic facilities.

But it looked as if I was going to have to stick it out. Ugghhhrrr, parents! I armed myself with my sponge bag and towel and crept to the door and listened. I opened it a chink. It was pitch dark. Nothing moved. Down below I could hear the eerie chimes of the clock striking eleven. I felt horribly alone. I didn't know where Matthilde's room was. Or her grandmother's.

Steeling myself, I launched into the darkness. I made it past all those spooky empty rooms to the bathroom, flung open the door and turned on the light. I washed, cleaned my teeth and survived the trip back with my heart thumping in my chest.

I closed my door firmly and leaned against it trying to get a grip on myself. The furniture loomed at me out of the gloom. An owl hooted. That did it! I made for the bed and dived inside. I pulled the bed curtains closed around me and slid down under the covers.

I don't want to go into that night. I'm ashamed to say I slept in my clothes — and with the light on. The house wasn't silent in the night. There were weird scrabblings from above and horrible echoey creaks from below. A branch of the creeper scratched constantly on the windowpane. And at one point I heard a crunching on the gravel outside and the sound of *chains dragging*.

I kept having nightmare visions of some Dracula-like figure climbing up the creeper outside. At any moment I could picture his great leering face appearing in the window, the light flashing on his pointed fangs! Escape through my bedroom door was out of the question. I'd have to run past all those empty bedrooms where, in my imagination, the white dustsheets took on strange shapes that rose and floated towards me in the darkness. And even if I made it outside I'd have to brave all those spooky trees as they clutched at me . . .

I hid my head under the pillow. There was no way I was ever going to get to sleep.

Chapter Four

The next thing I knew, I woke in total darkness feeling as if I was being smothered. I tentatively peeped out. Parting the bed curtains, I found light was streaming into the room. I checked my watch. It was eight a.m. To my amazement, I'd survived the night.

My room looked a lot less scary by daylight. I climbed out of bed and went to the window to confirm that night-time really was officially over. Down below, Titan and Sultan lazed on the gravel. As Sultan leaned over to give Titan a friendly lick, the chain by which he was attached to his kennel dragged along the ground. I felt very foolish indeed.

I could hear distant sounds from below. Reassuringly familiar sounds, like crockery being stacked and music from a radio. With a great wave of homesickness I thought of our kitchen back home. I could almost smell it. That familiar early morning burnt-toast smell. Mum had been saying for ages we ought to chuck the toaster out. But Dad insisted if you let the bread pop up twice you could get it just right. I could almost taste that burnt toast and marmalade mixture in my mouth. I wondered what Dad was doing right now.

Automatically I checked my mobile. There was a text from Jess.

night night sleep tight
mind the ghosties don't bite
jxxxxxxxxx

Ghosts? My fears of the night before seemed rather stupid now. The red wallpaper had quite a nice warm look to it by the light of day. I went over to the mantelpiece and stared in the blotchy mirror. God, I looked a wreck. Sleeping in your clothes makes even cold water appealing. I grabbed my towel and sponge bag and went to brave the bathroom.

To my surprise it was quite warm in there. The mirror over the basin was misted up. Someone had been in before me. I turned the taps on the monster bath and after a lot of hiccuping and gurgling a stream of hot water gushed out. So I had a hot deep bath which I lay in for quite a long time. This precious interlude of peace and luxury was disturbed by a rattling on the doorknob.

''Annah?' It was Matthilde.

'Oui?' (Notice how my French is improving!)

'Eskatoodessanpoorlapetidayjurnay?'

'Errrm?'

'Brekfuss!'

'Oh that, yep. OK, won't be a minute.'

Once downstairs, I went to the dining room to find no sign of breakfast. I tracked the sound of the radio to the kitchen. A large lady in an old-fashioned overall was leaning over the sink. She turned when I came in and dried her hands on a tea towel and came and shook me by the hand.

She gestured at herself. 'Florence,' she said.

I pointed at myself. 'Hannah.'

''Anna?' she repeated, the 'H', as ever, totally beyond the French.

I wondered if she was some relation, an aunt or some-thing. But she didn't bear the least resemblance to Madame de Lafitte or Marie-Christine. At any rate it seemed risky to call her by her first name so I decided to err on the safe side and call her 'madame'.

She pointed to some bowls on the kitchen table. 'Café ou chocolat?' she asked.

'Chocolat, s'il vous plaît, madame,' I replied. (Fluent French, you see – no worries.)

The remains of other people's breakfasts were strewn over the kitchen table. Unlike dinner it seemed breakfast was a casual affair that you could have when you wanted. Florence gestured to me to sit down. Within minutes she was pouring a stream of frothy hot chocolate into my bowl and had brought bread, butter and a pot of homemade raspberry jam. I spooned some jam on to my bread and as I took a bite I thought regretfully of the raspberry tart lying abandoned in Paris.

As I finished my breakfast, Madame de Lafitte came in with Matthilde. They seemed to be having a bit of an argument about something. Madame de Lafitte pointed towards the back kitchen and the name 'Edith' came up several times. I cottoned on that she was suggesting Matthilde cleaned out her cage.

Matthilde said something about me. When this riveting activity was planned, it seemed I was to be included.

I trailed behind Matthilde as she carried Edith in her cage and headed towards some outbuildings. She led me into a tumbledown barn. The place was strewn with sacks and musty boxes, mousetraps and rolls of barbed wire. There was a disgusting pile of muddy gumboots which Matthilde homed in on. She started searching through them, and finding a couple similar enough to make a pair, she passed them to me.

'Pour toi,' she said.

She stood by as I reluctantly took off my trainers. I gave each boot a good shake before I put it on. Wise precaution. A dehydrated spider and a load of mouse droppings fell out. The boots were far too big and made a horrible squelching noise as I walked. I stumbled along behind Matthilde as she led the way to some stables behind the château. They were currently unoccupied, but I could tell from the strong smell of manure that there must be horses around somewhere. Something told me that horses would be at the centre of my next humiliation. I'm rather scared of horses, particularly big ones.

Inside the stables, we filled a sack with clean straw and took it back to where we'd left the cage. We now had to relocate Edith in temporary accommodation. Matthilde seemed to have decided it would be good for Edith to have a fresh-grass diet and we spent ages trying to rig up a kind of outdoor guinea-pig enclosure with various boxes and grilles we found in one of the outbuildings. We made an awkward team as Matthilde insisted that everything had to be done her way. I tried to point out that it was a bad idea to tie everything with string. But Matthilde greeted my advice with a rolling of the eyes and shrugs of total non-comprehension, so in the end I gave up.

We had just got Edith settled, grazing contentedly in the enclosure with her cage emptied, washed out and set in the sun to dry, when there was a sound of a car coming up the drive.

Matthilde got to her feet shading her eyes and called out 'Grandpère' in delight. She ran across the lawn to greet an ancient mud-spattered Land Rover that came dragging a horse box behind it. The man who climbed out was tall and slightly stooped, balding on top with a pair of shaggy eyebrows that rose into a point, giving him a rather fierce appearance. I followed, standing back as a lot of hugging and kissing went on.

Monsieur de Lafitte then turned to me asking to be 'presented'.

I held back. This was the person who Mum had described as 'rather grand'. But he wasn't dressed in a grand way. He was wearing terribly shabby clothes: a worn old waistcoat and ancient corduroy trousers, gone at the knees, that Mum would have thrown out if they'd belonged to Dad.

'Bonjour, mademoiselle,' he said gravely, shaking me by the hand.

'Bonjour, monsieur,' I replied, careful to add the polite 'monsieur' as Mum had advised me.

'Très bien,' he said and cleared his throat, signalling us to stand aside.

Another man got down from the car whose job it appeared was to take care of the horse. He had a bit of a hunchback and eyes that went in different directions but he seemed to know what to do with horses. I stood well back, not wanting to get trodden on as he backed this huge black one down the ramp. Matthilde took the opportunity to show off her superior handling of animals. She went up to the horse totally fearlessly, petting it and rubbing its nose.

Monsieur de Lafitte turned to me once more and asked in English, 'So, do you 'unt? We will 'ave to find an 'orse for you.'

'Hunt?' I repeated. My hackles were rising. Typical French attitude – if it moves, kill it! Everything that was

British in me was shocked to the core. Besides, the nearest I'd ever come to riding was a donkey ride on the beach at Bognor Regis.

'No. I'm British. In Britain we've abolished hunting,' I said, feeling my face flush red.

He paused and looked at me seriously for a moment, then he knitted his brows with a fierce frown. 'I see. A young lady who speaks 'er mind!'

The horse started to play up at that point and he turned and said something to it in a commanding voice. The horse obviously knew who was master round here. It instantly calmed down and allowed itself to be led quietly towards the stables.

I went up to my room after that, wondering if I'd gone too far. I mean, by French standards what I had just said was probably terribly rude. And yet I had only spoken the truth. I *am* British and we *have* abolished hunting.

I reached for my phone in need of a comfortingly familiar voice and dialled up Jess's number. She'd be awake by now and I wanted to get a full account of the party.

'Hi?' Jess's voice sounded sleepy at the other end.

'Did I wake you?'

'It *is* Sunday morning.'

'Sorry.'

'It's OK. I'm awake now. You all right? What's all this about a haunted house?'

'Nightmare! We've been sent to the country.'

'No way! Why?'

'Not sure yet,' I lowered my voice. 'But I think Matthilde's mother is having an affair!'

'No *way*!'

'Umm.'

'How d'you know?'

'I saw her in a café with this man.'

'No way!'

'Umm. The way they were looking at each other, it was, I don't know, kind of *really intense*. At any rate there was something going on. That's why we've been sent here. Her mum has made off and left us in this huge, like, *château*.' I thought I'd lay it on a bit.

'*No way!*' Jess's responses were getting a little repetitive so I changed the subject. 'Anyway, how was the party?'

'Oh, you know.'

'I don't. You were there. I wasn't.'

'Yeah, well it was OK.'

'Umm?'

'Umm.'

'Did Mark turn up?'

'Umm.'

'So did you tell him I was in Paris?'

'Yep.'

'And what did he say?'

'He said, "Cool".'

'Cool?'

'Umm.'

'Is that all?'

'Pretty much.'

'Did he ask when I was coming back?'

'No.'

I paused while this sank in. He hadn't exactly broken down over the news.

'Then what did he do?'

'He asked if there was any lager.'

'Who did he dance with?'

'Pretty much everyone.'

'But who?'

'Do you want a list?'

Jess was being extremely uncommunicative. I decided to call it a day and try again when she was in a better mood.

'Look, I'll call you later, OK?'

'OK.'

After I rang off, I called up Angie. You always got the truth from Angie. She was the official class gossip. There's nothing she likes better than a good stir.

'Hi, Angie! How was the party?'

'Hannah! Too bad you missed it. It was great.'

'Oh?'

'Umm. God, you should see the mess! How's France?'

'It's still, you know, very French. Listen, Angie, did you speak to Mark last night?'

'Mark?'

'Mark Vincent.'

'Oh, him . . .'

'Did he ask about me?'

'Errm. He was kind of busy.'

'Busy?'

'Look, Hannah. I don't like to be the one to say this but . . .'

(Don't you just hate it when people start out like that?)

'Umm?'

'I thought Jess was meant to be your best friend.'

'She is.'

'Well, she didn't act like it last night . . .'

'She didn't?'

'Well, I don't want to be the one to say anything. But she and Mark seemed awfully pally. They left together. Maybe he was just being nice seeing her home, but . . .'

'Mark and Jess?' I paused while I got my mind around this.

'Looks like it. But honestly, I don't think it'll last.'

'Thanks, Angie. I knew I could count on you for the truth.'

'Loads more boys out there, Hannah.'

'Sure.' I clicked my mobile shut, feeling utterly miserable. Jess! Jess, of all people. And she knew how I felt about him.

My first impulse was to call her straight away and bawl her out. And then I thought better of it. I wouldn't call her. I'd maintain a dignified silence. She could call me up if and when she felt like it.

After that I lay back on my bed and did some deep philosophical soul-searching about boyfriends. Let's face it, they're a load of trouble really. I mean basically:

1) When you haven't got a boyfriend you worry like mad about being the only person in the world without one.

2) Once you have one, you worry about what your friends think of him.

3) If they think he's OK, you worry about losing him.

4) If they don't, you worry yourself sick about how to dump him.

5) Once you've dumped him, your friends never seem to think he was that bad after all.

6) The next thing you know he's going out with one of the girls who dissed him.

7) The whole cycle starts over again.

Sigh.

Lunch was a rather awkward meal. I guess I wasn't in my best mood. Old Oncle Charles greeted me as if he'd never seen me before and he *still* called me Caroline. Matthilde was behaving like the perfect granddaughter, passing dishes in strict order of ascendance and doing her sickly sweet 'oui-grandmère' and 'après-vous-grandpère' act. I didn't like to catch Monsieur de Lafitte's eye, as I was sure he was horribly offended by what I'd said about hunting. And then there was the matter of the stew.

Madame de Lafitte asked me at the beginning of the meal, ''Annah, est-que tu aimes la pain?'

Or at least, that's what I thought she'd said. 'Pain' is bread. I love bread, particularly French bread, so I replied in my best French, 'Oui, merci beaucoup.'

At that she ladled a big helping of stew on a plate and it was passed to me. I gazed down at it. There was a bone of some sort with meat on it, a bit like a chicken leg. But chickens didn't have claws like that. With a horrible sinking in the stomach, I realised that she'd been asking whether I liked 'lapin', as in rabbit.

I'd had a pet rabbit when I was little. Basically, what was on my plate was like a piece of *Flopsy*. I stared at it, feeling tears well in my eyes. The others set to, seeming not to notice. I nibbled at a piece of bread, wondering wildly if I could create a diversion and slip my portion to the dogs.

At that point, with the kind of fortunate timing that only happens a very few times in life, the telephone rang in the hallway. Madame de Lafitte put down her napkin and, rising from the table with a sigh, went to answer it.

I heard her voice change from a polite telephone-answering tone to one of concern. Monsieur de Lafitte got to his feet and went to the door and asked something. Even Matthilde went and joined him, standing behind and listening. There was a rapid fire of French conversation.

I glanced over at old Oncle Charles who at this particular moment seemed to have fallen asleep. In a flash I slipped my plate on to the floor and Titan – or was it Sultan? – was at it with one bound. There was just one enormous doggy slurp and my plate was wiped clean. I put it back in front of me and sat there with an innocent expression. The telephone call over, the three of them trailed back into the room and sat down. Monsieur and Madame de Lafitte had worried expressions on their faces but Matthilde for some reason had changed her mood entirely. She looked positively radiant. She actually nearly smiled.

Old Oncle Charles had woken up and was demanding to be told what was going on. They were all talking at once and I kept hearing the name 'Michelle'.

Madame de Lafitte looked over at me. She spotted my empty plate and with a bright smile she said, 'Mais oui, chérie. Tu aimes lapin!' Before I could stop her she ladled another big spoonful on to my plate.

This was even worse. The idea of eating rabbit off a dog-licked plate didn't bear thinking about.

I sat staring at it as Monsieur de Lafitte turned to me, saying in a not-too-cross voice, 'I go to get Michelle from the station this afternoon. If you like, you and Matthilde can come too.'

'Who's Michelle?' I asked.

'My cousin,' said Matthilde.

So this was why she was looking so pleased. No longer would she be stuck with me. She'd have another French girl to gang up with, probably one just as posey as her, if not more so. No doubt the two of them would be in a perpetual huddle speaking French at an impossible speed and I'd be totally left out.

I sat not eating with this dire prospect ahead of me. As Madame de Lafitte brought a salad to the table, I was embarrassed to see that everyone but me had a plate they'd wiped clean with their bread. It seemed you only got one plate in this house, but maybe that was because they didn't have a dishwasher. I was rescued by Madame de Lafitte. Catching sight of my plate, she leaned over and asked, 'Tu as terminée?', easily interpreted as 'Had I finished?'.

I nodded and to my relief she took my plate away and I was actually allowed a new one.

I rounded off my meal with as much salad and cheese as I could politely get my hands on. Luckily no one took any notice as the conversation continued around my head at a speed that was totally beyond me.

'Quel âge a Michelle?' I asked Matthilde as we took the dishes out to the kitchen to wash up. (Notice my other fluent French phrase.)

'Seize ans,' said Matthilde.

My heart sank. That did it. Sixteen. Almost the same age as Matthilde. This meant I'd definitely be left out.

I went to my room and rang Mum after that.

She answered right away. 'Poppet, you OK?'

'I s'pose so.'

'What's that meant to mean?'

'Honestly, Mum, you've no idea what it's like here. They had *rabbit* for lunch and Matthilde's grandparents are really strict and that old uncle still thinks I'm someone else. And there's a man who looks after the horses who looks like the Hunchback of Notre-Dame and he's really scary and . . .' It all came out in a rush.

'It can't be that bad . . .'

'It is. And what's worse, this cousin's coming to stay and she's the same age as Matthilde. I know they'll do everything together and I'll get totally left out.'

'Come on. Don't be such a pain. I've got so much on at this conference, you've no idea . . .'

'Can't I go home?'

'No you can't and that's final. You're going to have to put up with it. Two weeks isn't long.'

'Mum, there are still twelve whole days to go.'

'There's nothing I can do about it and you're *not* to bother your father.'

'I knew you wouldn't understand.'

'Listen to me, Hannah,' said Mum, putting her serious

voice on. This was getting heavy. 'You are there to learn French. If it's nothing else, this is a real opportunity to improve your language skills and you shouldn't waste it.' Then she rang off.

I stared at the phone feeling totally depressed. She never calls me Hannah unless she's really angry with me.

Grudgingly, I had to admit she had a point. If I was really stuck here, I might as well try to learn some French. It would come in handy with GCSEs looming. In fact, in spite of myself, I was making some sort of progress. I'd noticed that I was starting to hear individual words rather than a single stream of gobble-de-gook.

I raked through my backpack and located the French—English dictionary Mum had thoughtfully packed for me. I positioned it in the centre of the table. She'd bought me one of those little notebooks that have A–Z down the side as well. I got that out too and set it down beside the dictionary. It occurred to me that it might be prudent to list some of the trickier French words – I didn't want a repetition of lunchtime's disaster.

With a bold black marker I wrote on the front:

MY OWN PERSONAL PRIVATE FRENCH VOCABULARY

Then I turned to 'L' and made my first entry.

'Lapin – rabbit – not to be confused with *le* pain – bread.'

Dad rang me shortly after that. I could tell Mum had been on to him.

'Hi, Hannah. How's things?'

'Fine. I've written you a letter.'

'Uh huh? Not arrived yet.'

'I haven't posted it yet. How are you?'

'Bogged under.'

'Still marking exams?'

'Probably for days yet. So you're at Les Rochers?'

'Umm.'

'You don't sound too thrilled about it.'

'I'm not.'

'You do know some of it is thirteenth century?' (If anyone tells me that again, I'll scream!)

'Yes.'

'It was built to keep the British out.'

'Apart from me – apparently.'

'Hannah, honestly. The house is really historic. It dates back to the Hundred Years' War.'

'Humph.'

Dad then launched into one of his spiels, trotting out dates and kings and battles until my brain ached.

'I've got some really interesting stuff on the area somewhere, I could dig it out.'

'*Great.*'

Dad sighed. 'You don't know how painful it is to have a child who's a total philistine.'

'You don't know what a pain it is to have a dad who's a teacher.'

'Love you all the same.'

'I know. Parents are programmed to.'

Dad chuckled.

'Love you too,' I said.

Michelle was arriving by train from Paris at a place called Moulins. Monsieur de Lafitte suggested we went there early so we could have a look round, maybe have an ice cream in somewhere called the Grand Café. He said *ice cream* to me as if it was the biggest treat ever – like I was a little kid or something.

For some reason, Matthilde insisted she had to wash her hair before we left. I hung around downstairs waiting for her. She locked herself in the bathroom and was ages. Monsieur de Lafitte kept wandering into the hallway looking at his watch. In the end we only had time to make a last-minute dash for the train.

Matthilde seemed to be unusually agitated in the car, fussing with her hair and several times I caught her craning over to check her reflection in the rear-view mirror. For once, I noticed she'd actually put mascara on. Obviously out to impress her cousin, the way girls do, setting up a kind of private beauty contest between themselves. This thought depressed me even more. No doubt they'd spend the whole time holed up in her room, borrowing each other's clothes and trying out each other's make-up and sharing jokes that I was too young to be let in on. I'd simply be in the way – as if Matthilde hadn't made this plain enough already.

I sat in the back and stared despondently out of the car window as we drove through the streets of Moulins, wondering where all the cool shops were. According to Dad, it was a really historic town; Joan of Arc was meant to have stayed there on her way to fight the English. That figured, most of the buildings looked old and shabby enough to date back that far. I mean, basically, the whole place was crying out for a makeover.

A sign saying 'Gare s.n.c.f' pointed down yet another avenue of mutilated French trees and sure enough when we rounded the bend a typical squat little French station came into view.

A train was pulling out. I looked at it longingly. It was filled with luckier, happier people who weren't going to spend the next twelve days stranded in the country being treated like a lower branch of evolution by a pair of posey French girls.

Monsieur de Lafitte drove the car up practically on to the railway line. Then he and Matthilde leaped out and headed for the platform. I followed, preparing a mental picture of this precious Michelle. Hair – long and shiny. Legs – long enough for her to tower over me. Nose –

long enough for her to look down at me. Cheekbones — regulation French ones.

The train she was arriving on was due in at ten past four so we still had five minutes to spare. Matthilde eyed the letter I was carrying.

'Why you not post it?' she asked.

I'd been looking out for a postbox all through Moulins as we drove along but hadn't seen a sign of one.

'Where?' I asked.

She rolled her eyes and pointed to a box in the wall right beside where I was standing which I'd taken to be a rubbish bin. It seemed that the French couldn't have sensible postboxes painted red like the British. They had to be different and paint theirs *yellow*.

'Voici le train,' said Monsieur de Lafitte and sure enough, as I checked my watch, a train rounded a bend in the track and arrived dead on time. Which I grudgingly had to admit was another plus point to the French.

Matthilde was anxiously scanning the platform as people and bags and dogs and bikes and piles of postbags spilled out of the train. It was a long train and masses of travellers were getting off. Soon we were surrounded by a tangle of people greeting people, but there was no sign of Michelle.

Then suddenly Monsieur de Lafitte said, 'Ah, voilà!' and started waving towards the far end of the platform. Matthilde was waving too. In fact, jumping up and down and waving both arms. I stared despondently in that direction, expecting to see another picture-perfect Parisienne with her scarf tied in an oh-so-chic way. But the crowd had thinned and there was only a nun, a lady with a toddler and pushchair, and a tall dark, in fact rather gorgeous boy, carrying a backpack, with a guitar slung over one shoulder.

Monsieur de Lafitte took a few steps forward and flung his arms around this stranger, giving him a kiss on each cheek. Matthilde held back for a moment and then she kissed him too.

'Eh, jeteprésente 'Annah!' said Monsieur de Lafitte.

I looked up to find a pair of delectably dark eyes looking down at me. They were serious, unsmiling and deliciously flecked with gold. My heart went into a giddying free fall as I realised that we hadn't come to meet 'Michelle' at all – but *Michel*!

As he stepped forward, I took a step back, not sure of what to do. French adults you've never met before kiss you on both cheeks. But what about a total stranger who's a *boy*?

'Bonjour,' I said awkwardly. I could feel myself flushing scarlet. My step back seemed to have put Michel off balance. He seemed equally at a loss. He turned away and said something to his grandfather.

As the attention was taken off me, I made a gigantic effort to regain my normal colour. To my relief, the others were far too busy chatting to notice me. Monsieur de Lafitte kept an arm around Michel's shoulders and led us back to the car. There was a bit of a muddle as Matthilde suddenly didn't seem to mind being in the back of the car one bit. Maybe her legs had suddenly got shorter or something. At any rate I was allowed the front seat for once.

The drive back to Les Rochers gave me time to get myself back together again. Wow! Wait till I tell Jess about Michel! And then I remembered her and Mark. And that currently I wasn't calling her, because I was so outraged at her behaviour. But curiously enough the thought of Jess and Mark together didn't give me such a bad feeling any more.

No sooner had we arrived back at Les Rochers than a major drama broke out. Michel had barely had time to say 'Bonjour, Grandmère' to his grandmother and dump his backpack on the floor before Matthilde took him off outside somewhere, leaving me behind. She made it absolutely clear that I wasn't needed. In a rather haughty grown-up fashion, she indicated that I was expected to help her grandmother in the kitchen.

I went to the kitchen positively bristling with indignation. I was a guest here. I was the one who should be entertained and taken to see whatever it was in the garden. Instead, I was given the riveting job of laying the table for dinner. I was midway through my knife, fork, spoon, glass, napkin-in-its-little-bag routine when I heard a muffled scream from outside.

Madame de Lafitte hurried out of the kitchen drying her hands on her apron. I tracked her out through the front door heading in the direction of the scream. We found Matthilde standing over our makeshift outdoor cage. She wasn't looking grown-up any more. She had tears running down her face and her nose had gone red.

'Edith! EskavuzavayvuEdith?' she demanded.

One glance told me that our carefully constructed guinea-pig run had collapsed. Loose bits of gnawed string were scattered around. *Exactly* as I'd predicted.

Michel wasn't being very helpful. He mumbled something in which all I could understand was the word 'chien', meaning 'dog'.

'*Les chiens!*' gasped Matthilde.

The dogs were sitting at a respectful distance, although Sultan unfortunately was licking his lips.

'Mais non,' said Madame de Lafitte, springing to the dogs' defence.

Michel shrugged as if insisting he was right. Whereupon Matthilde shouted something at him.

What remained of the day was spent in a long exhausting session of 'hunt the guinea pig'. Michel joined in, in a half-hearted way, convinced as he was that Edith had ended up as a between-meal snack. This clearly made Matthilde furious and between snuffles and suppressed sobs, she snapped at him.

We searched the shrubbery and vegetable garden,

working our way through decaying greenhouses carpeted with shattered glass, crumbling outbuildings and the tumbledown barn which seemed like the storehouse for everything since the thirteenth century. Each of these was purpose-built as a guinea pig hideout. There were towers of guinea-pig-friendly flowerpots and loads of lumpy-looking sacks with guinea-pig-shaped contours. But search as we might under upturned buckets and through drainpipes of Edith's circumference, she was nowhere to be found. Eventually, we ended up in the stable beside a horribly smelly pile of used straw. It was positively rank and steaming.

Matthilde indicated the straw and handed Michel and me a pitchfork.

'Mais non!' Michel objected.

Matthilde stood her ground and they had a bit of an argument. Michel then stomped off, leaving us to it.

'Garçons!' said Matthilde to me contemptuously.

I nodded in agreement. Actually I didn't blame Michel; it was a filthy job and I couldn't really imagine finding Edith there anyway. But it was nice to have the privilege of being on Matthilde's side for once. Half an hour later we were exceedingly smelly and covered in straw but our search had proved fruitless.

Dinner that night was a somewhat livelier affair. Monsieur de Lafitte was in a communicative mood and I could see he was showing off telling Michel some long and incomprehensible story about something that was going on at his work in Paris. Old Oncle Charles made the occasional comment and I could see him catch Michel's eye with a twinkle from time to time. Nobody took much notice of Matthilde or me.

I think Matthilde was a bit peeved at being left out of the conversation. She compensated by being ultra-helpful. She kept leaping up from the table to fetch things from the kitchen and making a big show of walking round serving people. This was a bit of a change from the person who generally found it hard to haul herself out of an armchair. I noticed she'd put on her tightest jeans and some boots with heels that made her legs look even longer. Huh!

At the end of the meal I helped Matthilde take the dishes out. Monsieur de Lafitte had left a small amount on his plate and I hovered for a moment wondering if he was going to finish it. Eventually, when I could get a word into the conversation, I asked, using the new French phrase I'd carefully memorised, 'Tu as terminé?'

He looked at me aghast and then passed me his plate saying, 'Mais oui.'

I took away his plate wondering what I'd done. When I got to the kitchen, Matthilde told me in no uncertain terms that I could not call her grandfather 'tu'. I had made the most terrible error of politeness. Even she had to address him as 'vous', which is generally what you call teachers and strangers, not relations.

It really wasn't fair. I'd done my best to be polite and helpful and work my way through the minefield of French manners. But it seemed I'd offended Monsieur de Lafitte *again*.

In bed that night I updated my French checklist:

Negatives:

1) Food – like finding Flopsy on the menu.

2) Politeness – all that business about 'tu' and 'vous'. Trust the French to turn a word as neutral as 'you' into a brains test.

3) Le or la – even something as sexless as a dishcloth has to be 'masculine' or 'feminine'.

Positives:

1) Trains that actually run on time.

2) French BOYS! (Or one in particular.)

Chapter Five

The following morning, I thought Matthilde would want to continue looking for Edith but Michel hadn't come down for breakfast and she insisted we had to wait for him before we decided what to do for the day. She contented herself with leaving a bowl of Edith's favourite food in her open cage and placing it in a welcoming place inside the barn, well away from the dogs.

The large lady called Florence who had prepared breakfast for me the day before was back again. She made hot chocolate for me and Matthilde and then disappeared into the house. I heard the sound of a Hoover somewhere and came to the conclusion that she wasn't a relation at all but some kind of servant.

Matthilde didn't seem to want to move after breakfast. She hung around the kitchen reading her book, while Michel's bowl and knife and plate lay on the table waiting for him. I soon got bored and decided to go out and explore on my own. There was a door in the garden wall I hadn't been through and I wanted to see where it led.

The morning mist was clearing and I could just make out the sun, a brighter disc in the sky, trying to burst through. I wandered past the ruined greenhouses which skirted the outer perimeter wall. The door I'd seen wasn't locked and when I pushed it, it gave inwards with a creak. I found myself in an ancient orchard. The trees were leaning at odd angles, overgrown and knotted with age, but they still had the odd patch of blossom. There were fruit bushes too, and I caught sight of a load of strawberry plants that had gone to seed. In a sheltered spot up against the wall, I even found they had tiny strawberries growing on them — early ones — the first of the year, ages before they'd be ready in England. I bent down to pick one. It wasn't really ripe but I put it in my mouth all the same. It was like no strawberry I'd ever tasted — intensely flavoured between sweet and sharp.

That's when I was hit by something small and hard on the back. I turned and peered into the branches above me but couldn't see anything. Whatever it was must've dropped off the tree on to me. Spotting another strawberry, I stooped again and picked it and then found two or three more, riper ones this time, hidden under the leaves. Another tiny apple hurtled down and hit me.

'Ouch!'

Michel's face appeared through the branches overhead. In a single easy movement he swung down beside me.

'Bonjour, Rosbif,' he said.

Now 'Rosbif' is a really insulting way to address an English person. It means 'Roast Beef' — as if all English people are big and beefy. Mum used to get called it a lot when she was in France and it made her furious. However, it's pretty rude to call a French person a frog. So I replied, 'Bonjour, Grenouille.'

He looked at me very seriously. 'Toovoldayfrays?'

'What?'

'You steal straw-berries?' he said in pretty good English apart from his accent.

'No!' I said.

He took my hand from behind my back and opened it.

'Ah! One, two, three, four fraises. Tsk tsk tsk.'

I could feel myself flushing scarlet, not just because I'd been caught out but because he was standing so close. So close, I could feel the warmth of his body through the chill of the air.

He took a strawberry and threw it up and caught it in his mouth.

Then he held another out for me by the stalk. As I ate it, I felt myself go even redder. It was kind of embarrassing eating from his fingers like that. I knew I had turned the colour of roast beef — *rare roast beef*. And to make it worse, he was laughing at me. I could see he was. He was treating me like some little kid. I was thirteen and three-quarters, for godsake. At nearly fourteen I deserved more respect.

'No more.' I pointed to the strawberries growing at my feet. 'Pour Matthilde,' I said.

'Ah, pour Matthilde!' he said, as if this was the most important thing in the world. He broke off a couple of big flat rhubarb leaves with a flourish and handed me one. Then he began searching for the riper berries. I joined him. We worked our way through the strawberry bed finding more and more hidden from view. My leaf was almost overflowing when he indicated that we'd gathered enough and started to lead the way back to the house.

When we arrived at the kitchen door, Matthilde looked up from her book with a frown. She said something too fast to catch to Michel and he shrugged and went and sat at the table.

'Look, strawberries,' I said, holding them out to her.

Matthilde looked at them dismissively. 'Elles sont trop petites,' she said.

'No they're not, they're lovely, try one.'

But she was obviously in a bad mood. She messed around with pots and pans, making a big deal about heating milk for Michel's hot chocolate.

Michel ate in silence while she fussed over the cooker. I sat down at the table too.

'So what *are* we going to do today?' I asked.

'We ride ze 'orses,' said Matthilde.

'Oh . . .' I said, wondering how to admit I couldn't ride without sounding too lame. But as it happened this didn't matter as the 'we' Matthilde was referring to didn't include me. It was her and Michel.

I wasn't totally left out. My job was to open and close the gate for them. I hung around the stables waiting while Matthilde went upstairs to change. She came down dressed for the part – she had on a beautiful pair of shiny riding boots, really tight jodphurs and a polo neck under a smart little jacket. Michel didn't bother much, he seemed happy to ride in his jeans. I watched as he helped the cross-eyed man, who I'd privately nicknamed Quasimodo, to saddle the horses. I could see by the way he handled them, Michel knew what he was on about.

They were big strong horses and Matthilde needed Michel's help to swing herself up into the saddle. As soon as they were mounted, I opened the gate. I stood well aside, not wanting to get kicked or bitten or trodden on. Matthilde's horse did some frisky sort of sidestepping as it went through – the kind of thing that would have had me off and in the mud in no time, but she seemed totally unfazed. Then all of a sudden, they were off at a canter. I couldn't help thinking there was something intentional in the way Matthilde's horse flicked its tail at me as it turned into the lane.

Once they'd gone, I went back into the garden and wandered aimlessly. How I wished I'd gone to pony club. They might have been able to find something small and docile for me to ride. But maybe that would have been even more humiliating – me riding a pony while they were on those massive hunting horses.

During this depressing train of thought, I made a semicircle of the house and arrived back in the kitchen. I slumped down at the table wondering what to do with myself.

Florence came bustling into the room with the Hoover and found me sitting there. I think she sensed that I was at a loose end.

'Deedontuaytootserl?' she said, standing with her hands on her hips.

'Oui,' I said, since she seemed to be expecting a reply.

Then her eye was caught by our strawberries which were still on the table where we'd left them.

'Du jardin?' she asked.

I nodded. 'Oui.'

She then came out with a long sentence in which the only word I could catch was 'tart'. The very word brought back the thought of the poor abandoned raspberry tart in Paris and kind of compacted all the misery I felt. I fumbled in my pocket for a tissue. Florence stood for a moment staring at me, waiting for a reply. 'Toovermayday?'

I had no idea what she was going on about, so I tried 'oui' again.

At which point she went into the pantry and brought out a bag of flour and plonked a bowl in front of me.

'Noofaysonsoontart!' she said and started to measure out cupfuls of flour into the bowl. She continued rabbiting on with the word 'tart' cropping up a lot until it dawned on me that she was expecting me to help her make one. Big deal. Matthilde got to go out riding with Michel, dressed like some show-jumping star, and I was left behind *cooking*.

Having nothing better to do, I nodded grumpily. No doubt being French she would make a frightful palaver over it. I was right. It started with the pastry. I thought pastry came in packets and all you had to do was unroll it and shove it on top of pies. At least, Mum's pastry was like that. But it seemed that Florence had to delve back into the enigmatic origins of pastry. A total battle with butter and flour and water which had to be done quickly apparently. There was flour everywhere. However, I won and the pastry got rolled flat.

Florence then showed me how to flip it into the baking tin and crimp the edges so that it looked really professional. Then she flipped open the oven door and shoved it in.

I was about to slope quietly out of the kitchen, when she started going on about 'crème'. More palaver. You had to separate egg yolks from the whites by doing a kind of juggling act with the shells. I slopped one down the side of the bowl but she said it was 'pas grave' and scooped it up with a spoon.

She then took the bowl of egg yolks and stood it in a saucepan of water on the stove. Still no escape. My job continued with a hot, arm-breaking session of beating the yolks with sugar. Just as it started to thicken and I thought I was getting somewhere, she poured in hot milk and I had to beat even harder.

At this point Florence remembered the pastry and opened the oven to find it had gone all crispy and brown round the edges. The custard was poured in and we came to the artistic bit. I spent ages arranging the strawberries in perfectly regular circles on top. 'Voilà,' I said, as I positioned the final strawberry and prepared to make my exit.

Not so fast. Florence shook her head and waved a finger at me. She disappeared into the pantry and returned with a jar of shiny red transparent jam. More intensive stirring over a pan of boiling water. Then, with the aid of a brush, magically the strawberries looked like something out of an advertisement – scarlet, glossy and brilliant. I stood back. I couldn't help feeling a slight glow of achievement. If anything my tart looked even better than the one from the shop in Paris.

'Voilà!' said Florence. 'Ceswarpoor dessert,' she said and put a finger to her lips and went to hide it in the pantry.

The cooking session finished, I found myself at a loose end again. Another walk round the garden seemed the most promising event on my social calendar. I wandered round the flower-beds having a half-hearted look for Edith. Personally, if I belonged to Matthilde, I would have made myself scarce as well.

My tour took me round to a terrace that led out from the drawing room. The sun had well and truly broken through now and the terrace was bathed in warm sunshine. It was paved in stone slabs mossy with age, and half overgrown with flowers growing up between the cracks. An old rambling rose hung over it, dropping a snow of petals; you could smell it from miles off. A wicker chair had been set out in a sunny position and I could now see old Oncle Charles sitting in it. At least, I could see a battered panama hat and assumed he was under it, bent over his newspaper. He'd obviously nodded off.

I really didn't fancy another strange conversation in which I was meant to be someone else, so I tried to creep by quietly, hoping I could slip past without being spotted. No such luck. When I was midway across the terrace, the old man woke up with a kind of grunt and said, 'Caroline! Bonjour! How are you?'

'Very well thank you, monsieur.'

'Bring a chair. Come and join me.'

There was no escaping. I drew up a garden chair and sat down.

'So? You are alone?'

'Michel and Matthilde have gone out with the horses.'

'You don't like to ride?'

I shook my head. 'I don't know how to.'

'Huh!' said Monsieur de Lafitte. 'When I was in the States, they gave you horse. If you stayed on, you could ride.'

'When were you in America?' I asked.

'Took off at seventeen, worked my passage out. Didn't get back till after the war. New York, Chicago, Hollywood. Those were the days.'

'You were in Hollywood?'

He leaned towards me and said as if it was a big secret, 'I went there to get famous.'

'And did you?'

'Malheureusement no. But did I enjoy life?' He gave me a glimpse of his bright blue eyes.

'What made you go there?' I prompted.

'My father had plans for me.' He gave a dismissive look back at the château. 'I was meant to study law. Become an avocat – but I had different ideas.'

'What did you do in Hollywood?'

'Hung around the studios. Got hired by the day as an extra. Then I moved on to stunt work. Did stuff with horses.'

'You were in the movies?'

'Not so as you'd notice. Always got cast as an Indian 'cos I was skinny and dark.'

I stared at him, trying to imagine this old white-haired man dressed as an Indian galloping over the prairie.

'I was really good at having horses shot from under me.'

'No!'

'Not really shot. They train them to lie down. You have to get off double quick or you can have your leg bust. They like to get their own back, roll over on you. Pay was good though.'

'So why did you come back?'

'My father died. We had much land, many farms to manage. Mostly sold off now. Nothing left. Only this house and the park.'

He gazed out over the garden and seemed to fall into a reverie. His head nodded as if he was about to drop off again.

'Well, it's been really nice talking to you, monsieur.'

'Call me Charlie,' he said sleepily.

'Umm goodbye umm . . .' I said, getting up. I couldn't possibly call him Charlie. Madame de Lafitte would have a fit.

'So long, Caroline.'

I continued on my way wondering who was this mysterious Caroline? And why had he mistaken me for her?

I walked down to the meadow and strained my ears for the sound of horses' hoofs. I wondered where Michel and Matthilde had got to. They were having an awfully long ride. The thought of them out riding together made me seethe once again at the injustice of it all. By rights, I should be in Paris right now being taken on a luxury tour of all the sights. Instead I was stuck in the country working like some unpaid skivvy.

It gets worse. After lunch Madame de Lafitte produced a basket and handed me a pair of gloves and made it clear that she expected me to help her in the garden. Gardening! All that business of getting soil up your nails and thorns in your fingers and uhhhhhrrrr! But I didn't dare say no. Matthilde's grandmother was the sort of person you couldn't refuse.

Stiff with resentment, I followed her tall, straight back across the park to a rose bed. Madame de Lafitte didn't seem to notice my mood. She kept telling me the names of each rose in French and showed me how to prune them properly, counting the buds and cutting just above the second one that sticks out. She watched like a hawk until I got the hang of it. I snapped through each stem with determination. It's a good thing she didn't know the thoughts running through my mind as I decapitated her roses.

The sun got really warm during the afternoon. Matthilde and Michel still weren't back and I wondered rather unkindly whether Matthilde might be getting rather hot in her polo neck and jacket and jodphurs — which would jolly well serve her right.

At last I heard the approach of horses' hoofs at around four. Michel arrived first at a canter. I watched as he walked his horse slowly round the meadow. He looked pretty pleased with himself and I assumed they'd had a race. Matthilde came trotting up a few minutes later looking really hot and cross and Michel shouted something to her and roared with laughter. She slid down from her horse and threw the reins to Quasimodo and, without saying a word, went straight upstairs for a bath.

We'd finished pruning for the day and I went and watched as Michel and Quasimodo rubbed down the horses. It was a balmy kind of evening and it felt good just sitting there watching. At this time at home I'd normally be turning on the television, zapping through the channels, trying to find something worth watching. But that evening just doing nothing seemed OK.

Over dinner Monsieur de Lafitte turned to me and said that it was the last day of the hunt tomorrow, then his eyebrows bristled and he added abruptly, 'But you are British, so you will not come.'

Madame de Lafitte broke in, saying, 'Non, Gaspard, 'Annah viendra avec moi.' She turned to me, adding, 'We will follow with ze pique-nique.'

I looked from one to the other, caught between the fact that I should refuse to attend on principle, and curiosity about this ancient rite. I didn't desperately want to be left at home again with nothing to do. But I felt a bit anxious about *how* we were going to follow. Maybe they had other horses, ones I hadn't seen yet. I prayed they'd be really small and quiet and would follow nice and slowly.

Madame de Lafitte patted my hand quite kindly. 'We will not go near ze kill. Anyway, zey do not very often find anything to kill.'

I tried to put the hunt to the back of my mind. I kept thinking of how I was going to bring out the tart I'd made myself – well, sort of – for dessert. They seemed to take ages over the cheese. But at last Matthilde got up and started stacking the plates.

'No, wait!' I said and came out with the phrase I had been practising all afternoon. 'Nous avons *dessert*.'

'Ah-hah,' said old Oncle Charles and he unfolded his napkin again and made a big show of looking expectant.

I went to the pantry and returned with the tart. I placed it in the centre of the table. Madame de Lafitte came out with a great stream of French. Matthilde tried not to look impressed but I could see she was. Monsieur de Lafitte wanted to know where the strawberries had come from. Michel said something in which I heard the words: ''Annah et moi. Ce matin.' And I felt myself go hot and goose-pimply all over remembering the way he fed me that strawberry.

Matthilde gave him a hard look and then glared at the tart. She accepted 'un tout petit peu' and ate it in tiny forkfuls as if it was going to poison her.

The tart seemed to improve my rating somewhat with the others. Even Monsieur de Lafitte appeared to soften his attitude to me. Michel had bagged the biggest slice because he insisted he'd picked most of the strawberries. As he dug his fork into it, his mobile rang. Michel glanced down at it and then exclaimed, 'C'est Maman.'

These words produced an instant and dramatic change around the table. They all fell silent. Monsieur de Lafitte got to his feet.

Madame de Lafitte whispered, 'Reponds . . .'

Michel got up slowly and walked away from the table. I heard him say, 'Oui, Maman. Ouaytoo?'

If a serial killer had walked into the room touting a gun, you couldn't have felt more tension in the air. I watched Michel close his mobile as if in slow motion and turn back to the others.

'Elle va bien. Ellevootransmaydaybeesoo.'

This seemed a pretty short conversation for a mother.

Suddenly everyone was talking at once. Monsieur de Lafitte went and dialled a number on the house phone. Madame de Lafitte sank back into her chair and wiped tears from her eyes. Michel started dialling another number on his mobile.

Matthilde picked up a couple of dishes and signalled to me to follow her.

'What's going on?' I whispered once we were in the kitchen.

'Eez Michel's mother,' she whispered back. 'She 'as left 'eez father. They no know where she eez.'

'Oh,' I said. No wonder there had been so much drama. 'But that's awful.'

Matthilde tossed her hair. 'She will come back. Eez not the first time.'

'Really?'

Wow. So, I was right about French people. I had a sudden flashback of Marie-Christine with that man in the café – French women seemed to be worse than the men!

When I went back to clear the table, the others had all gone into the sitting room. The plate with Michel's portion of tart lay on the table with his fork beside it. He'd disappeared upstairs. He hadn't even touched it.

I went to my room after that feeling really peed off. There I was making a really big effort – I mean even cooking. And what happens – another drama. It was like living in a perpetual French film – all those big eyes and exaggerated gestures – *and* without subtitles. What I needed right now was a really nice *normal* girly chat. In a civilised language for once – like English. So I relented and called up Jess.

'Hi!' she answered right away.

'You haven't called in ages,' I said.

'Nor have you.'

'It costs a fortune from France,' I replied.

She made out that this was a feeble excuse.

'Anyway, you haven't called me.'

'I texted you.'

'I texted back.'

She was being really off with me. She was obviously feeling guilty about Mark and this was her way of covering up. So I came straight out with it:

'Angie said you and Mark left together the other night.'

'So?' she replied.

'So? Are you going out together?'

There was a pause.

'You can tell me. I don't care any more,' I prompted.

'I thought you were really keen on him.'

'No. Not any more.'

'So what's changed?'

I was about to blurt out to Jess about Michel. Not that there was much to tell. I mean the offering of one very small and not terribly ripe strawberry hardly amounts to a relationship. But something stopped me.

'I don't know. Just changed my mind, I guess. He's a bit young.'

'He's the same age as us.'

'Exactly.'

'Well, if you must know. Don't break your heart over it. His dad picked him up so I got a lift home. We live in the same direction.'

'And?'

'He said maybe we should meet up some time and he took my number.'

'And?'

'He hasn't phoned.'

I tried to suppress a tiny surge of triumph. I know I shouldn't feel like this. But it was a relief to know that someone else's love life was as uneventful as mine.

After that we had a good old goss in spite of the cost of the call.

I rang off wondering what I had been fussing about. You could forget Mark. Let him call her up, she was welcome to him. It was as if the whole Mark episode had been recorded over. I'd moved on. It was gone. Erased. For ever.

Later that night when I was trying to get to sleep, I heard Michel strumming moodily on his guitar. I opened my window to hear better.

His room was in the tower, up one floor above mine. The light shining from his window made a bright patch on my wall. From time to time, when he leaned into the window or something, his shadow loomed across it. It felt strange watching his shadow like that, close enough to touch, when he didn't know I was there.

Gradually, he seemed to calm down. He played really well. I listened as he played and sang a couple of songs. His voice reminded me a bit of the lead singer in Naff. Naff was a band Jess and I had come across by chance, fringe stuff not many people had heard of. But the lead singer had this voice that really sent, like, electric vibes through you.

Michel was singing in English and got a lot of the pronunciation wrong. But the way he was playing made me go tingly all over.

Thought for the day

Negatives:

1) The French are far too emotional — they can't be simply pleased or sorry or put out — they have to be 'ravi' or 'désolé' or 'derangé'.

Positives:

1) All that fuss they make about cooking — actually it's worth it.

2) The sound of a French boy trying to sing in English. Sigh.

Chapter Six

The following morning I came down to find the hunters had already left with the horses. Madame de Lafitte was busy with Florence, packing a huge wicker picnic hamper. I watched as jars of pâté and gherkins, a whole smoked ham and a cooked chicken were piled inside. It was going to be some 'pique-nique'.

Florence took the hamper out and stowed it in the boot of Madame de Lafitte's car. At the last minute Madame de Lafitte made a big fuss, insisting I got kitted out in gumboots, warning me that it was going to be a hard day.

One thing was clear. I was NOT going to spend the day squelching round in a pair of oversized wellingtons while Matthilde put herself about looking like something out of an ad in *Horse and Hound*.

I made a dash upstairs and took the new boots I'd bought for Angie's party out of my holdall. They were still wrapped in their tissue paper and they smelt deliciously of new leather. They were absolutely pristine, even the soles were still shiny. I'd only tried them on in the shop. As I slipped them on, I thought regretfully how they'd never got to the party in the end.

Madame de Lafitte frowned when she saw the boots and mumbled something I didn't understand. But I ignored this. As I climbed into her car, I wondered once again if I should have insisted on staying behind at Les Rochers as a protest. A voice in me that was sane and British and politically correct said I should. But there was this other voice that was arguing the other way. It had to do with traditions and all that stuff that Dad said was dying, and would only be in the history books and would never come back. And there was a third voice too, which said I jolly well wasn't going to be left behind *again* while Matthilde went off with Michel.

The road soon turned into a forest. The forest was vast, there were tall trees with straight trunks as far as the eye could see. Eventually Madame de Lafitte took a left turn down a dirt road which was rutted by car tracks. As we squelched through the puddles, I spotted a sign saying:

DANGER
Chasse à Cours

I sat in the car preparing myself mentally for the hunt. I tried to see things from the hunters' point of view – after all foxes are terribly cruel. They kill lambs – and you hear stories of them going through chicken runs savaging every bird in sight.

'I suppose it's a good thing to kill foxes,' I ventured to Madame de Lafitte.

'Foxes?' she said.

'Reynards?' I tried. I'd looked the word up in my dictionary.

'Oh, we do not 'unt foxes,' she said. 'We shoot *zem*. We 'unt deer and sanglier — wild pigs,' she said in a matter of fact way.

I stared at her in horror. I'd never quite recovered from that bit at the beginning of *Bambi*, when his mother got shot. And as for killing lovely stripy wild pigs — it didn't bear thinking about.

I stared out of the car window, my mind conjuring up noble visions of myself — standing arms outstretched defying the huntsmen. Or chaining myself to a tree in protest. Or lying flat out on the ground ready to get trampled on — this last one wasn't quite so appealing. I should have stocked up on liquorice — I could have laid a false trail. And then I imagined being found out by Monsieur de Lafitte and shamed in front of everyone and being sent back to England in disgrace.

We'd arrived at a clearing which was filled with cars and horseboxes. Men dressed in long green riding coats were clustered together. I spotted Monsieur de Lafitte smartly dressed in boots and riding breeches complete with a snowy white cravat with a pin with a crest on it. A man was letting a yelping seething mass of hounds out of a lorry.

The de Lafittes' ancient Land Rover was standing with its horse box open with Quasimodo backing one of the horses down the ramp. I caught sight of Matthilde already mounted, dressed immaculately as I'd predicted, in a tight fitted black jacket and a cravat like her grandfather's. She had her hair swept back into a neat little net under her riding hat. I noticed with some satisfaction that this time she was having quite a job controlling her horse, which was doing nervous sidesteps in its excitement.

Following Matthilde was another horse ridden by . . . Could it really be Michel? My heart did a wobble and turned over with a thump. He looked so tall on his horse, so gorgeous in his green jacket, although his cravat wasn't tied properly — it was practically hanging off actually — and his jacket didn't fit and was obviously borrowed from his grandfather, but he looked totally, totally yummy. He was like a younger version of those heroes of period dramas — kind of a clean-shaven Braveheart with Heathcliff overtones.

Madame de Lafitte, meanwhile, was drawing my attention to the hounds. They were arranged in a semicircle with four burly men standing in front of them. A man who Madame de Lafitte said was the Chief of the Hunt came out to the front. She explained that the four burly men were foresters — they'd been out since dawn checking for signs of animals and they had a special language for telling whether they had seen tracks or animals and where to find them. The hounds sat in their semicircle silently and obediently, ears cocked as if they were listening too and making a note of which direction they should set off in.

As soon as the foresters had finished their report some huntsmen with long hunting horns played a tuneless kind of fanfare and then, at a signal from the Chief of the Hunt, the hounds set off in a huge barking wagging mass with the horses hot on their heels.

I watched as Matthilde swept by without a glance in my direction. Michel was close behind her. I felt very small indeed. I wasn't dressed for the hunt. I was a lesser mortal in ordinary jeans and a Top Shop T-shirt. And at any moment I was going to have the humiliation of being forced to ride some pathetic clapped-out pony which I'd probably fall off.

Madame de Lafitte led me towards a smaller horse box. She opened it and I stood back expecting a furious snorting red-eyed pony to come charging out. But inside there were two bicycles.

OK, so I only had to follow the hunt on a bicycle. But you try pedalling on stony roads covered with slippery mud and a mush of dead leaves. My thigh muscles were soon screaming at this unaccustomed exercise.

As we rode, we could hear the hounds baying this way and that through the forest. We tried to keep up with the horses, cycling an odd circuitous route. There were a lot of about-turns from the huntsmen as they kept track of the hounds. Various different sounds rang out from the hunting horns, each – according to Madame de Lafitte – giving a specific message as to whether they'd sighted an animal or a broken branch or merely tracks. She cycled on in a stalwart fashion with me huffing and puffing behind to keep up. Horses are designed for slopes in a way that bikes aren't and we were forever going up and down. At one point Madame de Lafitte suggested we took a short cut to avoid a particularly muddy ditch. I agreed readily – anything to cut down on the thigh work. Big mistake! Madame de Lafitte's short cut was up a mini-mountainside. It was so steep we had to carry the bikes. Our feet slid helplessly on sticky clay and I kept losing my grip, descending with avalanches of loose pebbles.

I'd long ceased to worry about my leg muscles. It was the way my boots were suffering that really hurt. These boots had been designed for posing at parties (like Angie's) or maybe a quiet Saturday saunter down the mall. Instead they were getting gouged, deeply and painfully, by nasty jagged rocks. Mud was staining their nice natural calf colour a nasty cowpat brown. Brambles were adding the final touch, giving them an arty sort of cross-hatching from toe to knee.

At last we got to the top. Madame de Lafitte put down her bike, brushed herself off and patted her hair into place.

'Voici!' she said. She was barely out of breath. I was boiling hot and covered in mud and, what was worse, we had an audience. We'd arrived in a clearing and the huntsmen had got there before us. Most had dismounted and they were looking in our direction in cool and collected manner with not so much as a cravat out of place.

I felt every eye rest on me. Even the horses were staring at me in that haughty down-the-nose way of theirs. I shoved my bike behind a bush and tried to look as if it didn't belong to me. I could feel my fringe sticking to my forehead from sweat. I didn't dare look at my boots.

To my relief, neither Matthilde nor Michel was anywhere to be seen; they obviously hadn't arrived yet. Maybe I'd have a chance to get my breath back and run a comb through my hair before they appeared. No such luck. There was a quick exchange between Monsieur and Madame de Lafitte with the result that we had to cycle all the way back to get the car and fetch the picnic.

By the time we returned to the clearing, other cars had turned up and rugs were being laid out and little camping tables and chairs set up. Lunch it seemed was a serious matter. As I helped lay out the plates and knives and forks, I wondered miserably if my boots would ever recover from this terrible ordeal. It was difficult to tell what the damage was underneath all the mud.

Matthilde and Michel pitched up at that point and tethered their horses. Matthilde came over and threw herself down on a rug at some distance from us.

'Comjesuis fatiguée,' she groaned. Which I under-
stood. 'Fatiguée', like fatigue, meaning tired. *She* was
tired and she was actually on a mount which had four
legs and was doing all the work for her – not two wheels
and a rather rusty chain like me. I could hardly stand!

'Donmoykelkashosabwar,' she demanded to no one in
particular. Madame de Lafitte passed me a beaker of fizzy
water and indicated that I should take it over to
Matthilde. Which I did with difficulty. She was thirsty. *I*
could barely get to my feet.

Madame de Lafitte had piled a plate of food with prize
morsels and was holding it out. But Matthilde wouldn't
budge.

'Non,' she sighed. 'Jenepeuxpas – jesuistrop fatiguée
pour manger.'

Michel had plonked himself down on the rug next to
Monsieur de Lafitte's camping chair and was tucking in.
He observed Matthilde with a grin. He said something
that I interpreted as 'perhaps she couldn't take the pace
and should call it a day'.

Matthilde turned over with a pout and said something
back and they had a bit of an argument.

'Mes enfants,' exclaimed Madame de Lafitte, trying to
keep the peace. She started a big persuasion job on
Matthilde to eat something – as if she was going to die
of hunger during the afternoon if she didn't. I had
quietly helped myself to a prime plateful of roast chicken
and salad and was just about to take the first mouthful

when I was sent to deliver the plate to the exhausted huntress.

Over lunch the family became engrossed in a debate about the hunt. Monsieur de Lafitte turned to me and kindly translated. It seemed it was a matter of tactics; you didn't just charge after an animal, you had to manoeuvre the dogs so that they could surround it, then one of the huntsmen was meant to go in and kill it, quickly and cleanly with a sword.

'When the animal is killed the huntsmen skin it and chop it into pieces and cover it with the skin,' he said. 'Then the dogs are allowed in. After very little time they have eaten every single leetle bit, even the bones.'

'Oh,' I said. 'I thought we'd be having it for dinner.'

'No, no. That's another kind of 'unting. "Chasse à tir", with guns. 'Unted animals are full of adrenalin. Not good to eat.'

'Because they're so frightened,' I said, feeling myself go hot again with indignation.

'It is ze way in nature,' said Monsieur de Lafitte firmly. 'Animals 'unt other animals. At least they 'ave a good life first, living wild in ze forest. Perhaps not like ze chicken you are eating.'

I laid down the forkful of chicken I was about to put in my mouth. Suddenly I wasn't so hungry.

Now it was Madame de Lafitte's turn to remonstrate. She scolded her husband and I caught the words 'plein air' which meant that the chicken had been raised in the open air. 'Silly man. Soon no one will want to eat my picnic,' she said to me.

The afternoon was much like the morning. Loads of frantic chasing back and forth, baying of hounds and sounding of horns. But as Madame de Lafitte had predicted, the hunters never actually sighted an animal.

'It is a pity for ze last day of ze 'unt,' she said to me as we drove back to Les Rochers. I made no comment. I was only too glad the poor tormented creatures had survived the day to live a peaceful life until next season.

As soon as we arrived back at Les Rochers everyone went upstairs to change. Matthilde wanted first bath so I had to wait.

I took off my boots and tried to assess the damage. Mum was going to be livid. I'd really put the pressure on to get her to buy them. I'd even said they could be part of my birthday present, knowing of course she'd probably have forgotten by the time my birthday came. I scraped off most of the mud in the back kitchen and left them to dry, praying that time would work some sort of magic on them.

Matthilde was simply ages in the bath. The others had made their way downstairs while I was still waiting. I hovered on the landing with my towel and sponge bag. Wherever did I get the idea the French didn't wash? *If only!*

Below in the hallway I saw Michel checking the house phone for messages.

'C'est Papa,' I heard him say to Monsieur de Lafitte. Then he went into the study and dialled up a number. After that he had an angry conversation on the phone. I peered over the banisters from my hidden vantage point, wondering what was going on. He and his father were having a terrible row. I wasn't the only person eavesdropping. Monsieur de Lafitte stood in the hallway obviously listening in too.

I heard Michel slam the phone down and then Monsieur de Lafitte stormed into the room closing the door behind him. A terrific argument followed. Monsieur de Lafitte's normally deep voice was raised in anger. It was so loud I could hear every word through the door although I couldn't understand what he was saying. I heard Michel retort in a tone that sounded both rude and upset.

Suddenly the study door shot open and Michel dashed up the stairs two at a time. I shrank back in the corridor as he continued up to the second floor. His door slammed shut.

I wondered what the row was about. They were taking it pretty seriously. Matthilde came out of the bathroom at that point. She looked amazed at finding me standing there waiting and said I would 'ave to 'urry' if I was going to be in time for dinner.

Michel didn't come down for dinner, Madame de Lafitte went up with a plate of food for him and she stayed up there for ages. I had to eat with Monsieur de Lafitte and Matthilde and old Oncle Charles. Monsieur de Lafitte had an expression like thunder on his face and he cut the meat as if he was carving up an enemy. Neither Matthilde nor I dared say anything apart from 'oui' and 'merci'. Only old Oncle Charles seemed unaffected by the row. He ate steadily, giving Monsieur de Lafitte the occasional sideways glance, asking questions about the hunt, to which Monsieur de Lafitte replied in curt monosyllables.

The uncomfortable mood seemed to have seeped out into the house. Matthilde was quiet and uncommunicative and, as soon as we'd washed up, she slumped into a chair with a book. Oncle Charles went off to his room muttering to himself. Madame de Lafitte came down with Michel's tray and Monsieur de Lafitte immediately went with her into the study and closed the door.

The atmosphere made me feel like an intruder. I obviously wasn't going to be told what was going on, so I went up to my room and phoned Jess.

'How's France?' she asked.

'Horrid. I had to go hunting today and I totally trashed my new boots.'

'No! Not the brand new ones? Your mum's going to kill you.'

'I know.'

'Did you say you went hunting?'

'Umm. I'm not going to be able to walk tomorrow. It was agony.'

'You mean you were on a horse?'

'No. I was on a bike.'

'The French hunt on bikes?'

'No! Of course not. They were on horses. I was following them on the bike.'

I suddenly realised how naff this sounded.

'S.A.D.,' said Jess. 'What else have you been doing?'

My brain went through a lightning list of potential answers: a) Searching for a lost guinea pig, b) cooking, c) gardening, d) talking to a dotty old man. But none of these had quite the wow-factor I was searching for. So I said instead, 'There's been some sort of family row. But I don't know what it's about. Everyone's in a really weird mood.'

'When are you going back to Paris?'

'I don't think we are.'

'You mean you're going to be stuck in the country for the rest of the holiday?'

'Looks like it.'

'Nightmare, rather you than me.'

I felt somewhat peeved at her tone, so I asked rather pointedly, 'So? Has Mark rung you?'

'Not yet.' Jess then went into a long list of the brilliant things she had been up to, which included going to the cinema with Angie — the film wasn't that good. A planned shopping trip to the West End to spend her birthday money. And having her hair cut. I turned off actually as she continued through the predictable list.

As I put down the phone I had this sudden sense that it was all so far away. Like in another existence. Had my life actually been *that dull*?

After that I had a call from Dad. He sounded really excited. He'd found the 'interesting stuff' he'd been looking for, about the house.

'It was built for the de Rocher family. They were related to the Bourbon dukes,' he said.

'Re-ally?' I made a big show of sounding interested to please him.

'The Louis, the kings of France, are descended from them. There's even a rumour that one of the Dauphins actually stayed in the house.'

'Big deal. He probably had my bed. He didn't die in it by any chance, did he?'

'The Dauphin was the heir to the French throne, Hannah – they were generally young.'

'Might account for the dodgy springs then. He probably bounced on it.'

'I'm never going to interest you in history, am I?'

'Sorry, Dad.'

I made up for it by telling him about the hunt, which sent him into another excited monologue about French hunting traditions.

* * *

When he'd rung off, I lay on my bed staring at the ceiling thinking about all those people who had lived in this house before the de Lafittes. It wouldn't just be the owners, of course; there would have been servants too, countless maids and grooms, cooks and gardeners, washerwomen and stableboys. I tried to work out in my head how many people there would have been if you went back to the thirteenth century. Which makes the idea of ghosts pretty silly really. If all of them came back to haunt the place, it would be packed. Unless of course they were really thin, or transparent like they say ghosts are. Then you could get quite a lot in . . .

From above I could hear Michel strumming on his guitar. It was stuffy in the room and so I opened the window to let in some fresh air. Michel was playing the same song as the night before. Not in a showing-off way. You could tell he didn't know anyone was listening because he kept stopping and starting again to get things right. I left the window open so that I could hear him play. And I didn't fall asleep until he stopped.

Chapter Seven

The good weather continued. In fact it grew even hotter. The next day I woke to find the morning mist had already melted over the meadows. I heard a crunching on the drive below and saw Monsieur de Lafitte loading a suitcase into the back of his car. Madame de Lafitte was standing by; she handed him a raincoat, an umbrella and a briefcase — official-looking stuff that suggested he was going back to Paris. I watched as the car drove away down the avenue and turned on to the main road. It felt as if a weight had been taken from over my head. Monsieur de Lafitte had gone. Peace seemed to descend on the house.

I got dressed. It was going to be too hot for jeans so I put on the only really cool things I'd brought, a sleeveless T-shirt and shorts. Then I went down to check how my boots had fared during the night.

I found them standing where I'd left them on the draining board in the back kitchen. They'd practically dried out but there was a horribly white wavy tidemark where they'd got soaked. Sadly, I realised they'd never be the same again. Maybe I should tell Mum I'd lost them or they'd been stolen or something. Neither of which seemed very believable.

I had a half-hearted search along the shelves trying to find something to clean them with. Then it occurred to me that the place for this would be the stables. All the saddles and bridles were really shiny; they must polish them with something.

The room where they kept the harnesses was in a kind of lean-to barn attached to the stables. As I approached, I could hear someone at work in there. My heart sank. It was bound to be that scary-looking man who I'd nick-named Quasimodo. I hesitated and, as I did so, the door of the barn was flung open and Quasimodo lurched out carrying a saddle. He looked over and caught sight of me. Well, one of his eyes did.

'Bonjour, mademoiselle,' he said.

'Bonjour,' I said, wondering how I could make off without it seeming too odd.

He'd spotted the boots. Without a word, he limped over and took them from me. He turned them this way and that in the light making tutting noises.

I nodded. 'La chasse,' I said by way of explanation.

He shook his head again and lurched back into the barn with them.

I followed anxiously; maybe he was going to chuck them out.

But he laid out my boots gently on a bench like a patient about to undergo an operation. He nodded at me and said something that sounded like: 'Ay-ay-ay-ayben-noosallonvwar.' Then he reached for a little tin of something which he frothed up with a sponge like shaving foam.

I watched as he rubbed this foam in carefully. Then he put the boots out in the sun to dry. He pointed at his watch and made a sign with his fingers indicating twenty minutes.

I nodded. 'Merci, monsieur,' I said. At which point he broke into a great grin and said, 'Je jevousenprie – Narcisse.' He held out a hand for me to shake. It was as grained and rough as the bark of an old tree but warm and kindly all the same. He didn't look half so bad when he smiled. And you *could* tell when he was looking at you, it was just a matter of choosing the right eye.

'Merci, Monsieur Narcisse,' I said.

When I went back half an hour later, I found him with one of my boots on a special boot stand giving it the polish of its life with a folded cloth. The other was standing beside it, looking as good as new or maybe even better. I'd thought from the start they were a bit on the light side.

'Brilliant!' I said.

'May-may-may-cet un plaisir,' he said. And I realised that on top of everything the poor man had a stutter. I felt rather ashamed. It was really mean of me to be scared of him.

Michel didn't come down for breakfast and Matthilde and I hung around the garden wondering what to do. We went to the barn and checked Edith's cage but she still hadn't come back. Outside, the sun seemed to gain strength by the minute. The air was heavy and filled with the gentle buzz of insects. It was going to be too hot to do much.

We decided to make a sunbathing area down by the moat. I'd spotted a pile of decaying deckchairs and a wicker sunlounger in one of the outhouses. We set them up where the grass sloped down to the water's edge and managed to rig up a sun umbrella, which was kind of OK if you didn't sit under the torn bit.

The moat glinted invitingly. I went down to investigate. There were yellow flowers that looked like irises growing out of it and, as I leaned over, several frogs jumped in. A dragonfly did a long slow arc, its wings gleaming in iridescent blue and green. I dipped a hand in to test the temperature. The water was really cold but refreshing, so I slipped off my sandals and sat with my feet dangling in.

Matthilde had disappeared somewhere and she reappeared wearing a minimally body-covering bright pink bikini. Needless to say, she looked perfect in it. I reckon the French invented bikinis to humiliate people like me.

She asked me something which I took to be an enquiry as to whether I was going to change. I shook my head. I had my school swimsuit in my suitcase. It was a Speedo made for racing and not terribly flattering. Mum made me bring it, just in case we went to a swimming pool in Paris. I was *not* going to be seen in *that* beside Matthilde.

She wound her hair up into a neat knot on top, plugged in her iPod and laid herself out on the sunlounger. I sat feeling uncomfortably hot in my clothes, wishing I could sunbathe too. It was a bit lame sitting there fully dressed.

Time passed in a lazy sort of way – insects buzzing, frogs jumping, iPod tinkling and the occasional fish surfacing.

Then all of a sudden there was a massive SPLASH. Seconds later Michel appeared swimming strongly. He must have dived in and swum under the bridge. He hovered treading water in front of us.

'Bonjour, mes filles,' he said. He seemed to have totally recovered from his mood of the night before.

Matthilde glanced at him from over her sunglasses and turned over, which meant he got the treat of seeing her back view too.

'Come and swim,' he said to me. 'Ze water eez wonderfool.'

I shook my head. It was far too cold.

He put out a hand and splashed, so that a spray of icy water shot over Matthilde, drenching her.

'Deedon!' she exclaimed and sat bolt upright, dragging her towel round her looking really cross.

'Viens!' he called and splashed again.

He started fooling around, disappearing from sight underwater and re-emerging. His head appeared somewhat nearer. He splashed again. This time I got soaked. I leaned forward and splashed back. He surfaced by the edge and caught me by the ankle. I struggled and screamed but it was no use, slowly and surely I slid down the bank. Before I knew it I was in the water. It was so cold it took my breath away. There was nothing for it but to swim hard to try to get warm.

I cast a glance back at Matthilde. She'd wrapped herself in her towel and was glaring at us.

It was freezing in the water but not really weedy. The weed was an optical illusion – it was much further down. The effort of a few dozen strokes soon made me warm up and I decided to show off a bit. I was in the school swimming team and I can outrace most boys.

'OK, I'll race you,' I shouted at Michel. He dived under the water and swam away fast. I was after him like a shot and caught him by one foot. As I pulled him back, I quickly overtook. I glanced over my shoulder and saw his amazed face. I swam ahead easily to the end of the moat where there was a flight of stone steps. I hauled myself out and sat at the top on the sun-warmed stone waiting for him.

He climbed out. 'Not bad, 'Annah,' he said grudgingly. 'You swim fast.'

I nodded modestly. 'Oh, not that fast. Anyway my name's not Anna, it's Hannah.'

''Annah,' he repeated.

'No! *H*-annah!' I stressed the H for emphasis.

'H-Annah,' he tried.

'H-annah!' I corrected.

'H-annah,' he tried again.

I leaned closer showing him how to say 'H' by letting his breath out fast.

'H-annah.' He almost got it. Close up I couldn't help noticing he had nice teeth, really white and regular.

'Anyway,' he said. 'Why bozzer? I call you Rosbif.' He reached out and took a strand of weed out of my hair.

I turned and caught sight of Matthilde staring at us. She got to her feet and stomped off in the direction of the house.

'I better go and change,' I said.

Back in my room I dried off and changed into my swimsuit. I stared at myself in the mirror. It was so unfair. I reckon sports swimsuits are designed to flatten you. It's probably something to do with streamlining, so you can shoot through the water with the minimum resistance. I wished I had a bikini like Matthilde's. In fact I wished I had a body like Matthilde. And I'd have to do something about my hair. My hair is blonde and dead straight. Unless I've just washed it, it lies totally flat. And my fringe tends to stick to my forehead in a really unflattering way.

There was the sound of a hairdryer coming from down the corridor. I tracked the sound down it and found a door slightly open. So this was Matthilde's room. She was sitting on the edge of the bed drying her hair. Matthilde's room was nothing like mine. It had pink striped wallpaper and a little iron bed with a counterpane covered with a print of old-fashioned people. There were posters of horses all over the walls and an old cot full of dolls and teddies. You could tell this room had been hers ever since she was tiny, set aside and specially decorated for her by her grandparents.

'Can I come in?' I asked.

Matthilde nodded. 'Oui.'

It took a minute or two to explain that I wanted to borrow the dryer. Matthilde was having trouble blow-drying the back of her hair. I held out a hand offering to do it for her.

She passed the dryer to me. As I dried her hair, it turned back into her usual perfect glossy fall of bouncy hair. I would have given anything to have hair like that.

Matthilde was staring at me in the mirror. My eye caught hers.

'Michel eez like a leetle boy,' she said crossly.

'I know,' I agreed.

'You sink 'ee likes me?' Matthilde asked.

I hesitated. Anyone could see Michel thought Matthilde was a pain, behaving like such a princess. But on the other hand Matthilde was the kind of girl any boy would fancy. Most probably he fancied her like mad and was just covering up.

I replied diplomatically, 'Yes, of course he does. He's your cousin. He's practically like a brother.'

'But 'ee is not my brozzer,' she said, giving me a steady look.

'No, I know but . . .'

The way she said it, I could tell Matthilde was making it absolutely clear their relationship wasn't simply a family affair.

'You 'ave a boyfriend?' she asked.

I shook my head. 'No. Do you?'

'Not yet,' she said and a little secret smile played over her lips.

I finished drying her hair in silence. She'd made her point. Clearly Matthilde thought Michel was her property.

'Sank you,' she said with an eye-flick as she passed me the dryer. 'See you outside, OK?'

I finished blow-drying my hair staring at myself in the mirror, trying to see myself from Matthilde's point of view. Surely she didn't regard me as competition? Although I'm not *that* bad looking. I have the kind of English skin that people call 'peaches and cream', which I loathe personally. My best point is my blue eyes which are big like Mum's. But how I'd love to have cheekbones like Matthilde's. The French seem to be born with them. I reckon it's a kind of evolutionary thing – they've evolved them over generations by chewing their way through endless baguettes.

Humiliating or not, my shorts and T-shirt had to dry, so I was forced into wearing my swimsuit. I put a fresh

T-shirt on over it and went down to join Matthilde. She'd taken occupation of the one decent sunlounger and had dragged it down by the waterside. I noted that her skin looked a nice colour even before she was tanned. She had that lovely French olive skin that tans effortlessly, while mine goes scarlet at the very mention of sun.

I stripped off my T-shirt and stayed as much as possible under the parasol but it wasn't much help because of the holes. The day passed in a lazy sort of way. I needn't have worried about my swimsuit because Michel didn't want to join us. He went off somewhere on one of the bikes with the two dogs running behind.

Matthilde and I made sandwiches for lunch and ate them down by the moat. Matthilde picked all the ham out and threw the bread to the fish. She seemed cross and out of sorts and every time there was a sound on the gravel, she raised herself on one elbow to see if Michel had come back. I asked her where he'd gone and she just shrugged and said she didn't know.

Eventually, the sun went off our sunbathing area and Matthilde roused herself, shoved her sunglasses back on her head, took off her iPod, closed her book and headed back to the house.

I followed her, carrying most of our stuff. Back in my room, I stripped off my swimsuit and observed the damage. Although I'd rubbed in loads of sun cream, I could feel my skin tingling from too much exposure. I had hot red marks on my arms and shoulders. My face was scarlet and I could tell my nose was going to peel. I really did look like roast beef. Rare roast beef with seams of white where my swimsuit had been.

When Madame de Lafitte saw my sunburn, she made such a fuss I thought she was going to call an ambulance. She spoke quite severely to Matthilde and sent her to find some lotion. I had to sit still while she gently dabbed it over the red bits. It was lovely and cool and it did stop the stinging.

'Tomorrow,' she said, 'you wear many clothes and an 'at. No more sun.'

I went back to my room and caught sight of myself in the mirror. I've never seen such a fright. Madame's lotion had dried to an opaque white paste. I had a dead-white nose and two white blotches where my cheeks had been. I didn't want to go downstairs, Michel was back. I could see his bike abandoned on the lawn.

I don't want to go into the humiliation of dinner that night. I could tell everyone was trying to be polite and not notice what a sight I looked. But at one point I heard Matthilde whisper something to Michel which sounded like 'Pinochio' and she dissolved into giggles. Michel cracked up too, although he was trying not to show it. Madame de Lafitte put on her strictest expression and glared at them. I said I'd had enough to eat and went up to my room before we'd even had pudding.

I sat by my window miserably staring out. Why is it that when you want to look your most cool and sophisticated, disaster strikes? I only have to set eyes on a boy I like and I grow a monster zit, or I take it into my head to trim my fringe and end up looking like a moron. Uhhhrrrr!

I could see Michel in the garden below, making his way down to the moat. He started skimming flat stones on the water, the way boys do. Aw.

Hang on. Matthilde had wandered out on to the lawn. I watched intrigued as she approached Michel. Abruptly he swung round as he heard her.

She went and sat on the bridge, her legs swinging. I could see by the way she turned her head she was flirting with him. I wanted to drag myself away from the window but something kept me watching. Michel leaned towards Matthilde saying something back, then Matthilde bunked down from the wall and picked up a stone. She was trying to do ducks and drakes like Michel and clearly making a mess of it.

Michel picked up another stone, demonstrating to her how it should be done. Matthilde tried again, and messed it up. Then Michel went behind her, put his arm around her and guided her arm. I saw Matthilde turn her head and lean very close. A nasty flicker of envy ran through my body. I tried to suppress it. They'd known each other for ever, they were cousins, I reminded myself. But I remembered the way she'd looked at me when she said: 'Not yet.'

Chapter Eight

The following morning I woke up early feeling loads better. Whatever Madame de Lafitte's lotion had been, it had worked its magic; when I washed it off I found my sunburn had practically gone.

Matthilde was up early too. I caught sight of her beside the barn with the two bikes Madame de Lafitte and I had ridden at the hunt. The horses had been put out in the fields, now the hunting season was over, so the threat of riding no longer hung over me. I went and joined her.

'What are you doing?'

She frowned, her perfect brows raised in a perfect curve. 'Eez a good day to ride vélos.'

I didn't feel like pointing out there were only two of them. Madame de Lafitte had said I should stay out of the sun; clearly, if anyone was going to be left behind, it was me.

Matthilde spent some time fiddling round pumping up the tyres and then went into the kitchen. I followed and sat down at the table to eat breakfast. I could hear Matthilde in the back kitchen asking Florence for stuff; she seemed to be making a picnic.

Michel appeared at that point and slumped down at the table opposite me.

'Salut, Rosbif,' he said and made a grab for the last croissant.

'Salut, Grenouille,' I said.

He broke the croissant in two and passed me half. I took it and instantly forgave him for laughing last night — I must have looked really funny. Matthilde slid into a seat beside Michel and said something about the vélos. He shook his head in a very definite manner. Matthilde indicated the weather and the picnic and seemed to be doing a big persuasion job on him.

Michel turned to me. 'You want go out on vélos?'

'But there are only two.'

'I stay. I want to talk to Charlie.'

Matthilde looked cross and said something that I could only interpret as she'd taken a lot of trouble preparing the bikes. Michel shrugged and took a sip of his hot chocolate. He came up with a big frothy moustache and grinned at her from under it.

Matthilde pulled herself up to her full height and gave him a withering look. Then she turned to me and said huffily, 'OK, 'Annah, we go.' With that she strode out of the room with the picnic.

I had to dress up like a bag lady to go on the bike ride. Madame de Lafitte lent me a sunhat and insisted I wore a scarf tied round my neck and a long-sleeved sweatshirt over my T-shirt. I had to wear jeans and socks too and I was already pretty hot. As we rode down the avenue, I caught sight of Michel on the terrace drawing up a deckchair beside old Oncle Charles. It was nice of him to take trouble with the old man.

Matthilde had a cross, set look on her face. She pedalled in front of me as if her life depended on it and we were soon out on the open road. Predictably she was riding Madame de Lafitte's bike because it was bigger and her legs were longer than mine. They were and brown and gorgeous and were shown off at their very best in the shorts she was wearing. Madame de Lafitte's bike had gears and was reasonably new. Mine was the poor broken-down old thing I'd ridden at the hunt.

We pedalled down into the village. It wasn't much of a place, just a row of houses with a tiny church set back from the road. But there was a boulangerie, which had a throng of people going in and out in a typically French obsessive way as if their lives depended on a constant supply of fresh bread. My legs got a brief respite at the boulangerie while Matthilde went in and bought a baguette. I hovered outside with the bikes. You could hardly call the French standoffish, every single person who passed said 'bonjour'.

Soon we were off again down more country lanes. It was good cycling country, not too hilly and with practically no cars on the roads. But my bike wasn't exactly a candidate for the Tour de France. After a couple of hours of steady pedalling, I was hot and sweaty and longing for a drink. At last, at the end of a very long rise, Matthilde turned into a field and rested her bike against a tree.

She took a rug from her bicycle basket and spread it on the ground, then threw herself down on it. I parked my bike too and sat in the shade.

Matthilde turned over and looked at me.

'You are 'ot?'

'Very.'

Reluctantly, she got up and dragged the rug so that half was in the shade. I joined her and lay down too. It may not seem a particularly big gesture – dragging a rug into the shade. But it was the first tiny thing that Matthilde had done to register my existence and it felt like a milestone.

'I'll get the picnic,' I said.

I unpacked the things from the basket. There was a smoked sausage and a gooey Camembert at the ultimate point of ripeness, two boiled eggs and a couple of apples. She'd brought a big bottle of mineral water too and we took it in turns to drink out of the bottle.

As Matthilde passed me the bottle she said suddenly, 'You like Michel?'

'Yes, when he's in a good mood,' I said, feeling myself go even hotter under her gaze. 'He can be really funny.'

''Eez mother, ma tante, she eez really beautiful. She was a mannequin.'

'A model?'

Matthilde nodded. 'But she eez no good. She fight wiz my oncle. She make big problem.'

'Oh?'

Matthilde lay on her back and stared at the sky. 'I sink Michel eez like 'eez mother.'

'Really?'

''Ee's 'ow-you-say . . . mixed together?'

'Mixed up?'

'Oui.'

I thought of his angry strumming at the guitar. And his sudden changes of mood – she was right. But he could be really nice too. In fact, he was far nicer to me than most boys.

Matthilde's mobile rang at that point. She had a text message. She read it and then turned to me. 'Maman, she send you bisous. She is in the Dordogne,' she said.

'Oh?' It seemed an odd place to be working. The Dordogne was the kind of place people went for holidays. Or romantic mini-breaks!

'What's she doing there?'

'I do not know,' said Matthilde. 'But we cannot go back to Paris.'

'I see.'

'You want go back?' she asked.

I shook my head. 'No. Do you?'

'No,' said Matthilde with a smile. She stretched out luxuriously like a cat in the sun. 'Eez nice 'ere. Yes?'

'Yes,' I said and stretched out too. Matthilde had

relaxed, she'd dropped her Parisian posiness for once and was almost human.

It was even hotter in the afternoon. Matthilde said we were going round in a circle and we'd soon arrive back at Les Rochers. I pointed out that if we took one of the forest paths we could take a short cut and actually ride in the shade.

Matthilde agreed. 'Pourquoi pas?'

It was cooler in the dappled light and the paths had dried since the day of the hunt so the going wasn't so difficult. I spotted a lake through the trees and we went down to take a look at it. The water was cool and we dipped our feet in and lazed on the edge for a while. Matthilde found some flat pebbles and showed me how Michel had taught her to do ducks and drakes.

It became quite a competition actually. We were soon fighting over the best flat pebbles. Matthilde made totally over-the-top disparaging noises whenever I made a bad shot. But I was starting to get the drift of her Parisian humour. You had to give as good as you got. When her next stone sank without a single bounce, I did the same. Matthilde looked at me in surprise and then burst into laughter.

I noticed the sun was dipping behind the trees and when I checked my watch, I found it was way past six. Matthilde said it wasn't a problem, we just had to continue riding round the lake and we'd be home. But after half an hour or so we came to a marshy bit where the path abruptly stopped.

Matthilde looked really peed off and said something about it being my fault. I stood up for myself and said it was just as much her fault as mine; she was the one who knew her way around here. But whoever's fault, there was nothing for it but to cycle all the way back the way we'd come. The problem was all the forest paths looked the same. Eventually Matthilde slowed down, I came up beside her.

'I think we are "perdue",' I said.

'Oui,' she admitted.

'Perhaps we should ring your grandmother,' I said.

'Per'aps,' said Matthilde and got out her mobile. 'Oh zut,' she exclaimed, it needed recharging. 'But you 'ave yours, no?'

I shook my head. My mobile was really expensive to use in France. I was keeping calls to the minimum, so I'd left it behind.

'Why you not bring it?' said Matthilde angrily. She got back on her bike and started to pedal furiously.

It was getting dark and a cold dampness seemed to ooze from the trees. Matthilde was only in a T-shirt and shorts. At the top of a rise she stopped again. She was shivering and I could see goose-pimples standing up on her arms.

I took off the extra sweatshirt I'd been forced to wear and handed it to her.

'Merci, 'Annah,' she said and put it on. She actually looked grateful for once.

The forest all around us was really dark and I could hear strange rustlings in the bushes. I remembered the wild boar's head in the hallway at Les Rochers. I didn't fancy having a run-in with one of them.

'Eez OK,' said Matthilde, as if she'd read my mind. 'The wild animals — they run away from people.'

'How big is the forest?' I asked.

'Many, many kilometres,' she said and I could tell she was scared too.

We rode side by side after that. I wondered what would happen if we were forced to sleep the night in the forest. It was only April and the nights were cold.

We pedalled on steadily, in spite of being exhausted. At last I detected light up ahead. The trees started to thin out and we came to a wider path. We rode along this for a kilometre or so and then Matthilde slowed down and said, 'Ecoute!'

I listened. I could just detect the sound of a car. We heard it come nearer and then fade away in the distance. My heart rose — there must be a road up ahead. I could see Matthilde grinning at me through the darkness.

'Voilà!' she said.

We pedalled with renewed energy and at last came to the road. It was deserted.

Matthilde insisted that we should go left, but I had a gut feeling that Les Rochers was to the right. Matthilde shrugged then took a coin out of her pocket and said, 'Pile ou face?' Which was the French for 'heads or tails'.

'Face,' I said and won the toss, so right it was.

The road led on, looking silvery in the starlight. It was easier pedalling on tarmac and I started to have faith that we actually might see a bed that night.

We covered several kilometres and not a single person passed. Then Matthilde slowed to a stop and listened again. Faintly in the distance I could detect the sound of some sort of vehicle rumbling ahead of us. We put on a spurt and soon caught sight of the orange light swivelling round.

'Un tracteur,' called out Matthilde. By pedalling furiously we caught up with it.

It drew to a halt as we overtook it. I listened as Matthilde explained we were looking for Les Rochers. The driver replied in the guttural accent of the region, rolling his r's — impossible to understand. But he got down from the cab and piled the bikes on the back.

It was pitch-dark by the time we turned into the drive of Les Rochers. And there walking down the avenue in the gloom was a familiar figure carrying a torch — Michel.

The farmer pulled up outside the house and Michel helped us down. Matthilde practically fell in a heap into his arms, going on and on about the dreadful experience we'd had. I climbed down too exhausted to speak.

Madame de Lafitte came out of the house. She spoke to Matthilde quite sharply. It seemed French adults were just like English ones – they go right over-the-top when they're worried.

When I got up to my room I found I had a message on my mobile from my mother. I called her back.

'Mum?'

'How are you, poppet?'

'Fine. I just got back and found your message.'

'Back? It's late. Where from?'

'We went on a bike ride and got kind of lost.'

'Guess what? I've found I can change my ticket and stay over for the weekend. You can join me in Amsterdam. We could go to the Van Gogh Museum.'

'Van Gogh?'

'You know, the painter you love? Sunflowers?'

'I'm not so sure about sunflowers now. Aren't they a bit kind of corny?'

'He didn't *only* paint sunflowers.'

'Yes I know but . . . How would I get there?'

'By train. You can go via Lille. Change there.'

'Alone?'

'You could do it easily and you'll have your mobile. Then we can spend the weekend in Amsterdam and, if you want, you can come on home with me.'

'But I can't leave now.'

'Hang on. I thought you hated it there.'

'It's not that bad really.'

'Oh? So what's changed?'

'Nothing's changed. I've just got used to it, that's all. The weather's nice now.'

'And what's the cousin like?'

I hesitated. Mum had this embarrassing kind of second sight. Tell her the teensiest detail about some fanciable boy and she tends to go on and on about him.

So I just said, 'Not too bad.'

'And you're getting on better with Matthilde?'

'Kind of.'

'Oh well, in that case, by all means stay. But I thought you'd jump at the idea.'

'Maybe Dad would like to join you.'

'He's far too busy.'

'How's the conference?'

'Boring. It's about compressors.'

'What are they?'

'You wouldn't want to know. How's your French coming on?'

'OK, I think.'

'The big test is when you start to dream in French.'

'Dream! I don't think I'll ever get to that stage.'

She then went into a load of advice about learning phrases and trying to think in French. *Think* in French — as if speaking wasn't enough. But she dropped the idea of me going to Amsterdam. *Typical* of parents to try to drag you away once you've started enjoying yourself.

Chapter Nine

I woke next day to find a clear unbroken sky of pure forget-me-not blue. When I opened my window, the most incredible perfume wafted in. Seemingly overnight, the strange spooky vine had burst into life and long fronds of lilac-coloured flowers were curling over my window sill. Down the avenue, the trees weren't looking half so scary. A fuzz of frail green leaves was unfurling along the branches.

It had rained during the night and when I went down I found the garden all green and glittery. It smelt of new leaves and fresh grass. The rain had brought out a parade of snails who were gliding across the wet gravel. They had perfect striped shells and were the biggest, fattest snails I'd ever seen. I heard footsteps behind me and found Narcisse collecting them in a basket.

I continued on my walk down to the moat. It had risen a couple of inches during the night and, as I approached, there was a kind of synchronised diving session from the frogs. More yellow irises had come into bloom and the dragonfly of the day before had met up with several friends. They were hovering over the water like a convoy of miniature helicopters.

I wandered over the bridge and down the avenue keeping half an eye on Narcisse, who seemed to be gathering quite a harvest. Sure enough, when I returned from my walk, I found his basket plonked on the kitchen step filled with a highly mobile cargo. Up all sides of the basket, fat tortoiseshell snails were making a bid for freedom. This was France. I had a pretty good idea where those snails were going to end up. I was just about to help a few of them on their way when Florence came out and grabbed the basket by the handle.

She made some appreciative noises and filled a big flat terracotta bowl with bread and milk, by way of a last supper I imagined. I watched as she tipped the snails out into the bowl and covered it with a massive flowerpot. I decided to wait a while and, when she wasn't looking, liberate them in a field somewhere, a good long way from the kitchen.

It was too cold to sunbathe that day and Michel came up with the bright idea of playing tennis. There was a public court nearby and he said he'd seen some rackets somewhere.

Matthilde pointed out that there were three of us but Michel didn't seem to think this mattered. He went off to collect the rackets while we got changed. I laced up my trainers with some misgivings. I'd chosen netball rather than tennis at school, I bet the others would be really brilliant.

Predictably, Matthilde came down dressed for the part. She'd found a white T-shirt and shorts and looked ready for Wimbledon. Michel and I had to make do with our everyday jeans and T-shirts. He was carrying an old holdall with the rackets.

The court wasn't far off, half a kilometre or so down the main road, beside a municipal football field. As we approached, I saw a little old car parked beside the court and someone was knocking balls around – a lanky guy with ginger hair, a bit older than us.

'Oh, there's someone there already,' I pointed out. Maybe I'd be let off tennis after all.

Michel didn't seem concerned, he continued down the road.

Matthilde squeezed up her eyes and exclaimed, 'Ce'naypasvrai. C'est Arnaud.'

'Who's Arnaud?' I asked.

Matthilde did one of her over-the-top eye-rolls and said something that I could only interpret as: 'Don't ask.'

'A friend. 'Eez parents 'ave an 'ouse 'ere,' said Michel. He was soon shaking Arnaud by the hand and slapping him on the back. There was a quick exchange of French between them and then Arnaud turned to me.

'Bonjour,' he said. 'You are English?'

I nodded, 'Oui.'

I couldn't help noticing that Arnaud was dressed in immaculate tennis whites. He had hi-tech tennis shoes and one of the latest rackets. A brand-new Adidas sports bag lay on the ground with a box of bright yellow fluffy tennis balls beside it.

As Matthilde joined us, I noticed something else — it takes one to know one — Arnaud was a blusher. He had the kind of skin that turns red at the slightest cue. As he leaned forward to give Matthilde a kiss on both cheeks, his ears turned bright scarlet.

Matthilde gave Michel a look that could kill and Michel returned it with a wide grin. And I realised that this meeting was no accident. Michel must have set it up with Arnaud earlier.

Arnaud, still visibly recovering from greeting Matthilde, led us on to the court.

'OK,' said Michel, unzipping our holdall. 'On joue?'

I stared down at the choice of rackets. They were old wooden ones, somewhat warped, one of them had a string missing.

'We can't play with these,' I protested.

'Pourquoi pas?' asked Michel, gallantly taking the one with the broken string. Matthilde selected another with a set expression on her face and I took the last.

Arnaud was busy tossing a coin and getting us sorted into pairs. I was on his side and we won the toss to serve. Luckily, he was the one doing the serving; it wasn't my best stroke.

Four aces scorched across the court and Arnaud and I congratulated ourselves on one game to love. Then it was Michel's turn. The thing about a warped racket is that it makes each ball totally unpredictable. There followed the most hilarious game. Arnaud was rushing back and forth, covering the court while I stood glued to the spot, totally out of it. Game followed game and the others kept cracking up. But Arnaud insisted on stoically keeping the score, even contesting the occasional ball.

Anyone could see that Arnaud was showing off for Matthilde's benefit. But she was unimpressed. Half the time she wasn't even looking in his direction. He got more and more hot and bothered as she refused to take the game seriously. But how could anyone playing with rackets like ours? Michel, Matthilde and I soon had tears of laughter running down our faces. After a particularly brilliant, if purely accidental, drop-shot that completely floored Arnaud, Michel ended up flat on the ground, helpless with laughter. Arnaud paused, taking stock of the situation. He waited till Michel had recovered and then had a quiet word with him.

Arnaud seemed to think his services were ruling the game, so I was sent to the other side while he took on the three of us. Three to one, we were somewhat more evenly matched. We played on, changing the rules from time to time to allow for the curious behaviour of our rackets until we achieved something that vaguely resembled a match.

When at last we admitted defeat, Arnaud took his victory modestly. We tried to keep straight faces as he packed his gear into the car looking very pleased with himself.

As soon as he was out of earshot, we collapsed. I was laughing so hard it hurt. We walked back, hot, sweaty and with tummy muscles aching with laughter. I had to admit sport is bonding.

That evening Madame de Lafitte and old Oncle Charles went out to play bridge with some friends in Moulins. We were left to our own devices. We messed around in the kitchen making omelettes, competing over the most outrageous fillings. Michel insisted on having sardines in his. Disgusting!

Then after supper we played cards on the kitchen table for a bit. It was a game I didn't understand and I had a suspicion that Michel let me win once or twice. I was just about to turn in when Matthilde and Michel started talking animatedly about something and Matthilde disappeared upstairs.

Michel had found a torch and was signalling to me to come outside.

'Why, what for?' I asked.

He put a finger to his lips and turned off the kitchen light.

'Regarde,' he said, pointing at the sky.

I looked up and caught my breath. The stars were

shining as bright as fireworks. I'd never seen a sky like it. There were stars upon stars upon stars stretching away into infinity in giddying spirals.

Matthilde came out of the house carrying a rug. She seemed intent on taking Michel off somewhere. 'On y va?' she asked him.

He turned to her and said something about me. Matthilde shrugged and Michel insisted that I went with them.

There was a new moon that night. A tiny fragile arc that hardly gave any light, so it was the starlight that lit up the gardens. Out in the open it was so bright it actually cast shadows.

I followed intrigued as Michel led us across the lawn. We crossed the stone bridge and walked down the dark avenue of trees, Michel lighting the way with his torch. He pushed through a gap in the hedge, holding the branches back for us. We set off across the fields, soft grasses swishing against our bare legs. The air was filled with the spicy scent of the wild herbs we crushed under-foot. As we skirted the meadow, I became aware of night sounds all around us – soft flutterings and scrabblings in the hedgerows. Grasshoppers and moths darted in and out of the narrow torch beam.

Once through the meadow, the land sloped sharply upwards. We climbed for ten minutes or so. It was rocky and quite steep. We were all out of breath by the time we reached the top.

Michel spread the rug on the ground. I looked around, I could make out the dark shapes of trees far below and a ghostly herd of white cattle moving slowly through the gloom.

Michel pointed upwards.

'Etoiles filantes,' he said.

'What's that?' I asked.

'Stars zat fall,' he explained. 'We will see tonight. The first to see must make a wish.'

Matthilde had parked herself in the middle of the rug. Michel paused, looking down at her, and said something that must have meant 'budge over' because reluctantly she moved a few centimetres to her left. Michel settled down beside her and pulled me down too.

We lay on the rug, one on each side of Michel, staring up into the sky.

I shivered. There was something scary about the vastness of it all. We were looking up into space that went on and on for ever. I saw Matthilde reach over and take Michel's hand. And then he took mine in his other hand. His hand was warm; it was a boy's hand, strong and slightly rough, and it brought on another rush of that giddying free-fall feeling. Which I knew was stupid. He was only holding my hand in a brotherly fashion. It didn't mean anything.

The three of us lay there absolutely still — waiting. Minutes ticked by. My heart was thumping so loudly in my chest I felt sure the others must have noticed. I could hear their breathing and I could feel the warmth of them through the cooling air.

And then I saw a star falling so fast . . .

'Look!' I cried at exactly the same time as Matthilde called out, 'Regarde!'

'You must both wish,' said Michel.

I closed my eyes tight and made my wish. As I did so, I had the distinct impression that the two of us had wished the same thing.

That night my checklist came up with more positives.

Positives:

1) Hot weather. France seems to get much more of it.

2) Stars. They seem to have more of those too.

Negatives:

1) French boys. Not enough of them to go round.

Chapter Ten

The following day turned out to be Monsieur de Lafitte's birthday. He was coming home from Paris to celebrate. Madame de Lafitte was making a big fuss over the dinner and Florence was staying late to serve it. She was preparing all his favourite things.

In the morning Madame de Lafitte drove Matthilde and me into Moulins to buy presents. Matthilde spent ages in a bookshop and eventually chose a book about the history of hunting and had it wrapped as a 'cadeau' in special paper with a curly ribbon.

Then Madame de Lafitte took us into the most amazing chocolate shop. It was one of the poshest shops I've ever been in. It had a ceiling painted with roses and cherubs and all the chocolates were laid out in glass display cases as if they were really precious objects like jewellery or something. The ones she was buying had real gold leaf inside, which you could eat. Madame de Lafitte said it was meant to be good for you.

I watched as the chocolates were weighed out on old-fashioned scales and packed in a little gold-lined box with velvet on the outside. The assistant glanced at me with a smile and asked if I would like to 'goûter', which means 'taste'. I nodded and she passed Matthilde and me a chocolate each to try. It was dark and delicious and you'd never have known it had metal inside.

I'd counted through the euros I had and was wondering what I could possibly buy which would be grand enough to give to Monsieur de Lafitte. But Madame de Lafitte said he particularly liked English tea and we managed to track down a pack of Earl Grey tea bags in a shop that sold nothing but tea, every kind, including those horrible pee tea bags I'd had in Paris.

After that we actually did have an ice cream in the Grand Café. It wasn't all that grand actually. In fact, it was rather old and shabby. But all the walls were lined with mirrors in fancy gold frames. Where the mirrors faced each other, your reflection was reflected back at itself. I could see thousands and thousands of me, going on and on, eating endless ice creams, getting smaller and smaller as if I was trapped in a never-ending world of glass.

When we got back Florence was in a flap about the cooking. It was just a family meal but she was treating it as if royalty was visiting. Matthilde and I had to lay the table with a huge linen tablecloth and napkins with the de Lafitte monogram embroidered on them. The best china was taken out of the big oak cupboard in the salon. It was very heavy and also had the crest engraved on it in gold. Matthilde said it had been in the family for hundreds of years. Each place had to be laid with three glasses, two sets of knives and forks and a mysterious little implement that opened and closed like eyelash curlers with a miniature two-pronged fork.

Monsieur de Lafitte arrived at about five. He walked straight into the salon and said he wanted to talk to Michel. I offered to go and find him for him.

I searched the garden for ages and then it occurred to me he might be in the orchard. Pushing open the door, I called his name. There was no answer but I noticed a bird fly up with a cry of alarm from one of the trees. I went to investigate and found Michel sitting in a cleft in the trunk. He was whittling at a stick with a penknife and had an angry look on his face.

'Grandpère is here,' I called up.

'I know,' he called down, but didn't move.

'He wants to see you.'

Michel shrugged but still didn't make a move.

'You have to come down. It's his birthday.'

With a sigh, Michel swung himself down beside me.

'Où est-il?' he asked.

'Dans la maison.' I led the way back.

The minute Monsieur de Lafitte caught sight of Michel he took him into his study and closed the door.

Matthilde and I continued laying the table. We had to pass the study door as we went back and forth. I could see Matthilde lingering, trying to eavesdrop, but you couldn't hear words only the sound of voices from inside. Michel and Monsieur de Lafitte weren't talking angrily, their voices were low and serious.

Once the table was laid, we were banned from the kitchen as Florence fussed over her pots and pans. We had been told to dress up for dinner as it was a special occasion. I put on my one skirt and the strappy top I'd bought for Angie's party. I met Matthilde on the stairs. She had on a simple white dress that showed off her tan and she'd put her hair up and allowed little tendrils to escape. She looked really grown-up.

At eight o'clock sharp we were all assembled at the table. All of us that is apart from Michel. I felt a bit self-conscious in my top. Everyone else was pretty covered up. I could feel Madame de Lafitte's eyes resting on me uncomfortably. A semicircle of presents was arranged around Monsieur de Lafitte's place. He came in still wearing the smart suit he wore for work. He kissed Madame de Lafitte and Matthilde and me and slapped old Oncle Charles on the back.

Then he started fussing about the wine. Florence was sent to bring some special bottles up from the cellar. They were covered in dust and he opened these himself with a lot of ceremony. He placed a bottle on the table and sat down looking around expectantly.

'Où est Michel?' he asked.

No one seemed to know.

Monsieur de Lafitte then saw his presents and made a big show of looking surprised. He opened them one by one and made a lot of fuss. He even made some falsely appreciative noises over my box of tea bags. I mean, it wasn't much of a present really. I couldn't help noticing there was no present from Michel.

By this time it was eight-thirty. Florence kept glancing in from the kitchen to see if we were ready. She'd put on a fresh white apron, in place of her floral overall. She came and whispered something to Madame de Lafitte who raised an eyebrow at her husband.

'Non,' said Monsieur de Lafitte. He glanced around the table with a fierce expression on his face. 'Nous attendons.'

We sat and waited in silence. I could sense tension in the air. It was so quiet in the room you could hear the clock in the hall ticking. Ten or fifteen minutes went by.

Madame de Lafitte got to her feet and said she would go and look for him. But Monsieur de Lafitte wouldn't hear of it, he sent Matthilde instead. I had a pretty good idea Michel would be back in the orchard, so I offered to look too. I ran down the path and pushed open the door and made my way over to the tree. He wasn't there.

As I walked back to the house, I noticed something odd. There was only one horse in the meadow. I came face to face with Matthilde. We immediately went to check the harness room. One of the bridles was missing and a saddle had been taken from the saddle stand.

Matthilde frowned. 'Michel, 'ee will be in bad trouble,' she said.

There was a general murmur of disapproval as we reported back what we'd seen.

'Alors,' said Monsieur de Lafitte, flicking out his napkin angrily. 'On commence.'

There was dead silence at the table as he poured some wine into his glass, swilled it round and held it up to the light. Then he sniffed it and took a big mouthful and made slurping noises. We watched as he put the glass down and said, 'Bon.'

He poured some into old Oncle Charles's glass, who sipped it and put his head on one side and raised an eyebrow thoughtfully and then nodded to Monsieur de Lafitte who half filled his glass. Matthilde and I were given a spoonful to taste. Nobody drank their wine, I noticed. It just sat on the table while we waited for our food.

I felt really miserable seeing Michel's chair empty. At an eye-flick from Madame de Lafitte, Florence came and took away his plate and serviette and knives and forks. She returned with tiny plates that looked like the palettes you mix watercolours on. They gave off a strong smell of hot butter and garlic. A little plate was placed before me and I recognised six of those snails I'd promised to liberate. They were foot up, hot and steaming in butter and parsley. Seeing them like that somehow summed up the misery of that meal.

Everyone apart from me started tucking in, behaving as if everything was perfectly normal. I fiddled with my bread and nibbled at a crust. The others were too busy talking but Oncle Charles noticed I wasn't eating. 'You don't want?' he whispered. I shook my head. And his hand stretched out and he deftly switched his plate of empty shells for mine.

After this there was something called 'kennels'. They were long and white and flabby in a pink sauce that tasted of mud. I had a little nibble at one and got a mouthful of what felt like semolina, which I loathe. It really makes me gag. Old Oncle Charles noticed this too and, while nobody was looking, these mysteriously shifted from my plate to his.

The others ate and chatted as if Michel didn't exist. But my mind kept swerving back to him. How could they all be so unfeeling? I was worried about him. He'd galloped off in a mood. Maybe he'd had an accident, been thrown or something and was lying in a ditch somewhere with a broken leg or arm or *neck*.

The next dish was tiny birds still with their heads on. Mine were positively staring at me. I put my knife and fork down and said I wasn't hungry. Which was true — having your food watching you is enough to put anyone off.

I couldn't even fill up on dessert. There was a bowl of cherries to round off the meal. So all I had of this grand celebration meal was some salad, a small piece of cheese and a handful of cherries.

But I didn't feel like food anyway. I felt utterly wretched about Michel. He was only making things worse for himself.

Eventually Matthilde signalled to me to start clearing away the dishes.

'What's going on?' I asked when we were alone together.

Matthilde glanced towards Florence who was in the back kitchen.

'Grandpère eez angry because Michel 'as 'ad a big quarrel with eez father,' she said.

'What about?'

She shrugged. 'About lycée. 'Eez father make 'im study classics, 'e no want.'

'Oh? Can't he decide for himself?'

'I do not know,' she said. 'Eez ve-ry important. Eez his future.'

That evening no further comment was made about Michel. We had coffee in the salon in tiny china cups and Monsieur de Lafitte passed his special box of chocolates around. I didn't even have the heart to eat chocolate, so you can see how I was suffering.

I was passing Oncle Charles his coffee when we heard a door slam and footsteps in the hallway. Matthilde got to her feet and was about to go to the door when Monsieur de Lafitte told her abruptly to sit down and stay where she was.

He said to me, 'Toi aussi, 'Annah.'

Matthilde and I exchanged glances as her grandfather strode out into the hall. He said something brusquely to Michel and then we heard Michel's footsteps continuing up the stairs.

Monsieur de Lafitte came back into the room and closed the door firmly behind him. He called Matthilde over and had a quiet word with her.

She explained to me later that Michel was in disgrace and had been sent to his room and we were not allowed to speak to him.

The row had spread a gloomy atmosphere so I went to bed early. I lay staring up at the ceiling. There was no sound from above. Michel was evidently too angry or miserable to play his guitar. It all seemed pretty heavy to me. I mean, what precisely had Michel done? He'd missed a meal – admittedly on Monsieur de Lafitte's birthday. But they seemed to be making a real drama over it.

How I wished I could creep up and comfort him. But there was no way I could risk disobeying Monsieur de Lafitte.

Some time in the middle of the night I woke up absolutely ravenous. I checked my watch. It was three a.m. Hours and hours to go till breakfast time. I lay there tossing and turning and trying to ignore my hunger pangs. But at last I had to admit that I simply wouldn't get back to sleep unless I ate something. I dragged my jeans and a sweater over my pyjamas and ventured out into the corridor. I hurried past the empty rooms and crept down the main staircase. Just as I was crossing the hallway, I noticed a light coming from under the door of Monsieur de Lafitte's study. I could hear voices on the other side. Who could be up at this hour? I crept closer to listen.

A voice distinctly said, 'In all the towns in all the world, she walks into mine . . .' Whoever was in there was speaking English! I turned the handle very, very quietly, intending to take a tiny peek. It was the television I could hear. There was an old black and white movie on, and Michel was sprawled on the sofa in front of it.

He caught sight of me and put the film on 'hold'.

'Rosbif!' he whispered. 'Come in.'

I crept in and closed the door behind me.

'Where did you go? Why didn't you come to dinner?' I whispered.

He shrugged. 'I did not want to celebrate wiz my grandfather. It was better not to be 'ow you say – 'ypocrite?'

'But he was really angry.'

'What did 'ee do?'

'Nothing. They just ate dinner, like you didn't exist.'

Michel shrugged again. 'That is what 'ee is like.'

He turned back to the film moodily and flicked the remote control on to 'play'.

I hovered, watching the flickering images on the screen. Then I made to leave. As I turned the doorknob, Michel said, 'Wait. Can you 'elp? They speak too fast. I do not understand.'

I paused. It was risky. To be caught up in the middle of the night with Michel, when we'd been strictly instructed not to speak to him, was defying Monsieur de Lafitte. However, the temptation to stay when Michel had actually asked me to help was pretty irresistible. And they were all being so mean to him. He patted a seat on the sofa. I went and joined him. But I didn't sit right next to him. I sat a good way off, near the other arm.

The film he was watching was an old VHS, and there was a pile of cassettes beside him. He put the film on rewind.

'Where did you get all these movies?' I asked.

'They belong to Charlie. 'Ee 'as many. Old movies. Vintage American. A big collection.'

The film he was watching was called *Casablanca*. By the grainy texture of the print, you could tell it was really old. He explained that it was about all these people running away during the Second World War. They wanted to get to America but were stranded in Casablanca which is a town in North Africa. Everyone was trying to buy visas illegally. There was this really beautiful woman who was trying to leave with her husband. She didn't seem to care much about her husband. She was in love with another man called Rick, who was being horrid to her. But you could tell it was because he loved her really and he was trying not to show it. It was really emotional. I could feel tears stinging in my eyes. Michel wanted me to explain the dialogue, which was difficult with the big lump I had in my throat.

The bits he didn't understand came mainly from the character called Rick. He talked in a deadpan way out of the side of his mouth, never giving so much as a twitch of expression to show if he was joking or not.

It was about four a.m. when the film came to an end. I'd been so wrapped up in it, I'd quite forgotten I was hungry.

As Michel rewound the video, I admitted I'd come on a pantry raid. He said he was ravenous too, so we crept like burglars through the house to the kitchen. We didn't dare put the light on and had to find our way by touch. Every time we made the slightest sound we froze.

The pantry door opened with an alarming creak but Michel fumbled round and located a baguette. There was a bowl of strawberries too.

'Et voilà,' said Michel. 'Tartines aux fraises!'

'What's that?'

'Regarde,' he said.

He poured some strawberries on to a plate and kind of mashed them with some sugar. Then he took a piece of bread and split and buttered it. He spread on the strawberry mixture and made a big squidgy sandwich. He passed it to me. I took a bite. My mouth filled with the delicious sensation of bread and butter and strawberries.

'Yummy,' I whispered.

Michel nodded, his mouth was too full to say anything. He did a little drum roll on the plate with the knife by way of accepting the praise. It made me think of one of the songs I'd heard him singing.

'That song you were playing the other night. It reminded me a bit of a British band – Naff.'

'Oh?' said Michel. 'I do not know. They are good?'

'Brilliant.'

'Really?'

'I've got three of their CDs with me.'

'I can 'ear?'

'I'll lend them to you.'

We went upstairs after that. Feeling our way on tiptoe through the hall in the darkness. We kept bumping into things and I got a fit of the giggles from the tension of it all. I could tell Michel was trying to suppress the urge to laugh too. I was glad Matthilde wasn't around, she would have given us one of her haughty looks and told us we were being childish.

The trip up the stairs in silence was even more diffi-cult. We took off our shoes and crept up barefoot. Michel went first, and I padded up behind him trying to avoid the squeaky boards.

When we reached my bedroom door, I whispered, 'Wait a minute, I'll get the CDs.'

I fumbled for them in my holdall, then crept back to the door.

I could just make out Michel's silhouette in the gloom. I handed over the CDs and as I did so he caught me by the hand.

He whispered, 'Bonne nuit, H-annah.'

It was pitch-dark in the corridor and as I turned my face towards him for the usual mwah-mwah on both cheeks, I must've turned the wrong side or something because the kiss sort of landed in the middle, *right on the lips*. I mean, it was probably a mistake and if so *really* embarrassing. But on the other hand *maybe it wasn't a mistake*.

At any rate I kind of floated into my room and closed the door behind me. I leaned on the door with my heart thumping in my chest, trying to work out what had happened. And I realised he hadn't called me Rosbif, he'd actually called me Hannah and made a big effort over the 'H'. That must mean something, mustn't it?

I lay awake in bed for ages after that, going over everything that had happened that evening. My mind kept returning to the film. It made me think of Marie-Christine and the stranger in the café. Maybe I'd been rather hard on them. I mean, love is *such* a powerful thing.

* * *

Update of my checklist:

Positives:

1) French boys who are able to recognise life beyond football, like vintage films and fringe bands and things.

Negatives:

1) Snails.

2) 'Kennels' in pink yuck sauce.

3) Food that looks you in the eye.

Chapter Eleven

When I woke the next day, I had the memory of the night before still fresh in my mind. That kiss — had it or hadn't it been for real? Everything that was positive and optimistic and confident in me said it had. All that was mean and negative and self-critical said it was *a totally embarrassing mistake*. Eventually, I hauled myself out of bed to check the weather.

The sky was once again a clear unbroken blue, it was going to be a perfect day. I threw open my window and leaned out. Some bird was making an odd wild cry. I rested on the sill and watched as it rose effortlessly, climbing higher and higher in the sky. It was a huge bird with tattered ends to its wings, it looked like an eagle. Abruptly it paused and hovered with its wings outstretched. It seemed to hang there, held weightlessly on the up-draughts. Then, taking slow and easy circles, it spiralled down. It made me think of flying dreams, that fabulous feeling of finding you can fly and being up high, miles above everything and everyone, held safely by the wind.

I dragged myself from the window and forced myself to get dressed after that. Downstairs, the heavy front doors of the house had been left open to allow the sun in. The sunshine slanted across the hallway lighting up the dark corners and turning the stone a creamy golden colour. Even the stags' heads looked cheerful in the sunlight. The moose actually had an optimistic gleam in its eye.

Florence came out of the kitchen humming to herself and told me my breakfast was on the table. I could see from an empty yogurt pot that Matthilde had already had hers and disappeared somewhere. But a bowl and knife and spoon was still waiting for Michel.

I was on my third 'tartine' when Michel arrived. I didn't dare look at him after that kiss. I could feel the start of a mega-blush spreading up from my neck. He sat down at the table with a brief: 'Bonjour, Rosbif.'

I sneaked a glance, trying to gauge some reaction. He reached for the bread as if nothing had happened. His sole communication consisted of grunts about passing the jam or sugar or more slices of bread.

Matthilde appeared in the kitchen doorway carrying a bunch of wild flowers. She took one look at Michel and snapped something about 'hier soir', which meant yesterday evening. What with 'the kiss' and everything I'd totally forgotten about the row. I wondered what would happen next between him and Monsieur de Lafitte. Knowing my luck, Michel would probably be sent home.

Michel didn't reply. He just reached for another piece of bread and continued eating. Matthilde plonked her flowers in a jug and started arranging them delicately one by one, talking in a rather prim fashion as she did so. The word 'grandpère' came up several times. But Michel didn't react. Eventually he got up from his seat and took his empty bowl to the sink, saying abruptly to Matthilde, 'C'est mon affair. Toontekoop.'

She turned and caught me watching her. Then she frowned, swept up the jug of flowers and went off to her room.

Michel watched her go with a raised eyebrow. Then he came back to the table and sat down. He reached into his pocket and brought out the three CDs I'd lent him.

He placed them, one by one, in front of me.

'Well?' I asked, wondering wildly what he thought of them.

He looked at me with a perfectly straight face and said, 'Incroyable.'

I looked at him doubtfully. 'You don't like?'

'No! I say "incroyable" — 'ow you say mind-blooming!'

'Mind-blowing!'

'Yes!'

We then went into a long mutual fan session about the band. I think I impressed the socks off him by telling him I'd actually got hold of a white label of theirs that hadn't been released yet.

* * *

After breakfast I went and stretched out on the one good sunlounger, which was free for once. I settled down with a sunhat over my face to keep out the glare. I felt incredibly lazy, even ready to doze off. I hadn't had that much sleep the night before. I could hear the faint sound of Florence's radio coming from the kitchen and the *clip clip clip* of shears as Narcisse trimmed the hedge. The hat smelt deliciously of hot straw and, when I closed my eyes, little swirling patterns of red and green danced across my visual field.

I lay there reliving that moment in the corridor last night. In my new version – the action-replay of the kiss – it had been intentional. In fact, it was even better in slow motion. It lingered rather longer than the original.

I felt a shadow fall across me. The hat was lifted off. Matthilde stood over me looking bored and out of sorts. Obviously, I wasn't going to get any peace.

'Eef you lie there you will be burned,' she said.

'I've put on loads of sun cream.'

'Grandmère wants us to go to ze market.'

True enough, Madame de Lafitte was walking across the lawn with a basket in her hand. She wanted us to buy eggs from a particular farmer. It seemed we were expected to walk there. Matthilde was just doing a big moan about it being too far when Michel emerged from the house, coming up behind his grandmother.

Madame de Lafitte turned and a few words were exchanged. I expected she was going to give Michel a hard time about the night before, but instead she gave him a kiss on both cheeks and handed him the basket. I had a sneaking suspicion that she was providing Michel with an excuse to get out of the way while his grandfather calmed down.

Michel seemed only too happy to walk to the village. He turned to me and said briefly, 'Tu viens avec moi?'

He'd said 'tu', which clearly meant that he was only asking *me* to go with him, not Matthilde. I got to my feet expectantly. All of a sudden Matthilde didn't think it was so far any more. She took the purse from her grandmother and asked what else she wanted us to buy.

We took a short cut leading across the fields. A path led alongside the moat and we soon came to a weir where the river fed fresh water into it. Michel showed off a bit walking along the top of the weir the way boys do, making it look twice as dangerous as it was. I pretended to ignore him but Matthilde made a big fuss about him slipping off and getting drowned.

Our path soon branched away from the river and led between meadows with cows in them. We had to climb a fence and Matthilde wanted to be helped over. It was a pretty easy fence actually and I swung over it with no problem.

Michel raised an eyebrow as he lifted Matthilde down and then he winked at me and made a big play at pretending he'd put his back out, which made her furious. She didn't have any trouble getting over the next fence.

As we walked along, I hoped Michel wouldn't mention the film we'd watched the night before and he didn't. But the two of us kept yawning and Matthilde gave us a curious look.

Our route took us through a field full of young bullocks and they started following us. Matthilde and Michel were obviously used to cows and didn't seem to worry. But I could hear their hoofs pounding on the ground behind me. The hairs rose on the back of my neck as the sound of their hoofs and even their breathing drew closer. Every impulse told me to run. I was making a dash for the fence when Michel caught me by the arm and swung me round to face them. To my intense relief the bullocks backed off in a huddle looking stupid.

Matthilde was in fits. 'Pauvre 'Annah. Elle avait peur,' she said, pretending to be amazed that I should be scared. It was her turn to exchange glances with Michel this time.

'No I wasn't,' I lied. But I guess when it comes to making fools of ourselves, Matthilde and I were now one-all.

The village was in a festive mood when we arrived. Accordion music was being played over loudspeakers and stalls with bright awnings had been set out on either side of the street. There were people selling clothes and bric-a-brac as well as fruit and vegetables and there was a man who kept bees who had a display of honey and soap and beeswax candles. I bought a bar of handmade soap that smelt of chocolate for Mum and looked around the market for something to take home for Dad. Eventually I settled on a smoked sausage crusted with chillies.

The farmer we bought the eggs from had a crate of newborn chicks. Matthilde wanted to buy one to make up for not having Edith. But Michel insisted it wouldn't be fair bringing up a chicken in a Paris flat. They had a bit of an argument about it.

Once we'd done the round of the stalls, Michel said he was going to treat us to a drink in the café. The bar was full of farmers in muddy boots drinking red wine. The place smelt of cigarette smoke and garlic and cows. There was a low buzz of French voices punctuated by the occasional burst of rough laughter. Matthilde and Michel spent a long time deciding what we were going to drink and eventually settled on a bright green syrup which the barman topped up with fizzy water and ice cubes.

We took our drinks outside and sat at a table in the sun. As I took my first sip, Michel lifted his glass and chinked it against mine and said, ''Ere's looking at you, kid', which was a quote from the film we'd watched. The way he looked at me over the glass made me think that the kiss last night hadn't been a mistake at all. I felt myself going hot and cold all over.

Matthilde noticed and frowned, saying, 'Quoi?' Michel mumbled something about it being from a film, which seemed to satisfy her.

The green drink tasted oddly of peppermint and I know that, as long as I live, I will never ever taste peppermint without thinking of that moment.

I'd finished my drink and was savouring the lingering minty taste and the warmth of the sun when a car drew up and hooted at us. Matthilde shaded her eyes and then said, 'Mais nonsaypajoost, c'est Arnaud!'

Arnaud climbed out of the car and came over to our table. He shook Michel by the hand and kissed both of us and stood awkwardly waiting to be invited to join us.

Matthilde got up from her seat and gave me a hard look, making it plain that we were about to leave. I grabbed the basket and got up too.

Arnaud took the basket, saying, 'You want me drive you back to Les Rochers?'

Michel nodded. 'Pourquoi pas?' He went and opened the front passenger door for Matthilde, and put the basket on her lap. He paused and said to me, 'I think, 'Annah, we like to walk, no?'

Arnaud climbed into the driving seat with a grin. 'D'accord. A bientôt.'

As they drove off Matthilde sent a resentful look in our direction. Poor Arnaud. Matthilde was not the ideal person to have a crush on.

'I 'ope you like to walk,' said Michel.

'Oui, oh yes, that's fine,' I said, trying to sound casual, trying to ignore the little tingles of anticipation that were running up and down my spine.

'Arnaud, 'ee like Matthilde,' he said by way of explanation.

'So I noticed.'

We walked on in silence for a while, my mind racing. Had Michel actually suggested we walk back together to have some time alone with me? Or was he simply giving Arnaud a break? I scrutinised him out of the corner of my eye. He walked at some distance, idly kicking a stone, giving no indication of one or the other.

Then abruptly he broke the silence, asking, 'You 'ave seen my grandfather today?'

I shook my head. 'No. He must have gone out before I was up.'

He kicked another stone, harder this time.

I could sense that he wanted to talk about the row of the night before, so I prompted, 'Matthilde said the argument was about school.'

Michel nodded. 'My father 'ee want me study classics, old stuff, so to become a lawyer.'

'And you don't want to?'

'Eez so boring. Can you imagine? You must learn all these books. That means hours and hours at a desk . . .'

'And your grandfather, he wants that too?'

Michel nodded. 'My father 'ee send me 'ere to think it over.'

'I see.'

He started walking faster. I practically had to run to keep up with him. 'So what do you want to do?'

He continued at that speed, staring hard at the ground. 'What I want is to learn electronics, infotech, stuff that is useful . . .'

'Useful for what?'

He slowed down, talking earnestly now. 'You really want to know? I want to work in films.'

I stared at him. 'Doing what?'

He shrugged. 'Actor, director, lighting, camera, I don't mind . . . anything.'

'But films are really difficult to get into.'

'I know. But all this study is a waste of time. I can start at the studios, doing leetle jobs, 'elping out.'

'But your father wouldn't like that?'

He frowned angrily. 'They want me to go the Grandes Ecoles. 'Ave a profession.'

'My dad's a teacher. He says it's best to let people choose their own career, that way they work harder.'

'In France eez not the same. You 'ave to learn all ze boring 'istory, philosophy, classics, to 'ave respect.'

'Isn't there anyone on your side? What about your mother?'

'My mother agree with me. It make big trouble. That eez also problem. They say eez my fault.'

'I suppose your parents want what's best for you,' I said, hoping to calm him down.

He swung round abruptly to face me. 'Even you, you do not understand!'

'Well yes, I do. At least I think I do. It's just what you want to do is so *difficult.*'

'Then I try, I work. I make it 'appen,' he said stubbornly.

'Maybe,' I said haltingly, 'you could do something with your music.'

He flushed with pride. 'Last year, when I was on 'oliday in the Midi, we 'ad a soirée in a restaurant. A smart place – Le Dauphin. I made up a song for a friend and when I play it, ze manager 'ee say I was so good I could play professional . . .'

'Professionally?'

'Yes. If I was in England or in America, it would be different. But my family . . .'

He shrugged and started walking again. I hurried after him. 'Well, whatever they think, I'm on your side.'

He kicked angrily at another stone and missed it, catching his toe and stumbling forward clumsily to land on all fours.

I had to stifle a laugh at that. 'Maybe you could be a comedian,' I suggested. 'A sort of French Mr Bean.'

He got to his feet rubbing the mud off his jeans, still looking angry. Then he made a teasing grab at me with filthy hands. I ran off with a shriek. We weren't that far from Les Rochers. I was up and over a fence before he could catch me. We arrived at the house hot and out of breath. Thankfully the race seemed to have blown away Michel's angry mood.

We found Matthilde in the kitchen crossly unpacking the basket.

'Où est Arnaud?' asked Michel innocently.

Matthilde took an egg out of the basket and threatened him with it. Michel grinned at her and went off whistling to himself.

'Poor Arnaud,' I said. 'He's quite nice really.'

''Ee is like a big lost dog, always coming 'ere,' she said. She left me to finish unpacking the basket and stomped off to her room.

That evening I had a call from Jess.

'Hi, how's things? What you been up to?' she asked.

'Not much. We went for a walk to the village and bought stuff.'

'*Walked?*'

'Yes.'

'What about the cousin? Has she arrived?'

'Yes. But she's not a *she*. She's a *he*.'

'A boy? Sixteen! *What's he like?*'

'He's OK.'

'Come on, you can do better than that. Tall? Short? Fit? Eyebrows that meet in the middle?'

'No, he's fine. He's quite tall, dark and, umm, he's into movies.'

'Like what?'

'Old ones. Black and white.'

'*Old* movies?'

'Yes.'

'He sounds weird.'

'He's not. He's just French. French boys are different.'

'You can say that again.'

'He's into cool music too – he likes Naff.'

Jess started on a spiel, wanting to know exactly how he'd heard of them and which songs etc.

'Look, I've got to go or I'll be late down for dinner,' I interrupted her.

'Dinner. You mean you have to be on time?'

'Yes. We have proper sit-down meals here.'

'The whole family?'

'Yes.'

'Without the telly on?'

'Yes!'

'Rather you than me.'

Jess rang off after that. Suddenly, I remembered her house. They had a TV in every room and they were all on all the time. I couldn't recall ever sitting down to a meal with her family. We just helped ourselves from the fridge when we were hungry.

Over dinner that night everyone seemed to be fussing about the following morning. Madame de Lafitte leaned over and asked me, '`Annah, est-que tu viens à la messe avec nous demain?'

'La messe?'

'Mass. It is Easter Sunday,' she explained. 'A really important fête.'

I hadn't realised the week had gone by so fast. Easter Sunday already. At home it would have meant hot cross buns for breakfast, an Easter egg hunt in the garden and then gorging on chocolate all day. We never went to church.

'But I'm not a Catholic,' I said by way of an excuse. I was rather nervous about church, all that standing up and sitting down at the right time and finding your page in the prayer book. And in French too. I was sure I'd make a total idiot of myself.

'You must come,' said Madame de Lafitte. 'All day I 'ave been 'elping with the flowers. The church eet looks beautiful.'

It seemed rude to refuse so I nodded and said, 'Oui. Merci beaucoup.'

'Très bien,' said Madame de Lafitte. 'Et Michel?' She turned to him.

'Non, Grandmère,' he said and came out with a stream of French that seemed to displease everyone.

Madame de Lafitte replied with a long speech in which the name Jesus cropped up a few times but Michel shrugged and replied briefly with a sentence in which I recognised the word 'superstition'.

The following morning I woke early. I checked my watch. It was seven a.m. I'd been told we would go to mass before breakfast. I dressed quickly and went to the window to find the weather had changed. A light drizzle was falling. It was quite cool.

There was some sort of commotion going on outside. Something had disturbed the dogs. I saw one of them come bounding across the lawn barking fit to bust and then the other joined him. Someone was throwing a stick for them. As I leaned out, I saw Michel approaching from the far end of the park. He must have woken even earlier than me.

I watched as he and the dogs started a silly game. He'd pretend to throw the stick in one direction without letting go, then he'd throw it in another. It took a moment or two for the dogs to catch on. Sultan was much brighter than Titan. After a few false starts, he crouched down and waited with a big doggy smile on his face to see where the stick would really go, while Titan went hurtling off in the wrong direction. But Michel was being fair to Titan, he wasn't going to humiliate him. He threw a few easy sticks in his direction and made a big fuss of him when he brought them back. I watched intrigued.

It was on one of these forays that Titan disappeared beneath a low-growing bush. He stayed there ages and Michel started whistling at him. For some reason he wouldn't come out and I could see the bush swaying as he scrambled round under it. The dog emerged with some-thing that looked like a large fluffy tennis ball in his mouth.

Oh-my-god! It was Edith! I raced down the stairs and forced open the big oak door and found Michel kneeling on the ground beside the dog. Titan was sitting with a great lopsided grin on his face looking really pleased with himself.

'Regarde,' said Michel. 'Edith. Elle va bien.'

Edith was nibbling at the lawn in a nonchalant fashion. She walked a few steps and then turned back to look at us with a blade of grass sticking out of her mouth.

'Wow, Matthilde will be so happy!' I said, reaching down and picking her up. I was about to run up to Matthilde's room with her when Michel said, 'Wait, I 'ave idea.'

He put a finger to his lips. 'Do not say Matthilde any-sing. Promise!'

I felt this was a bit mean, it was probably another of his big teases. But sharing a secret made us feel closer somehow. So I went along with it.

'OK.'

Michel disappeared with Edith in the direction of the barn.

When I returned to the hall, I found the others had all come down. They were dressed in their Sunday best. Even old Oncle Charles had a smart coat over his usual sagging jacket and baggy trousers.

'You will need a coat, 'Annah. It will be cold in the church,' Madame de Lafitte warned me. Reluctantly, I went upstairs and returned in my school coat. To my surprise the coat was greeted with murmurs of admiration. Even Matthilde agreed.

'Beautiful. Eet is so English. Is it Scottish tweed?'

The French never cease to amaze me. Apparently they thought my coat was terribly chic, in fact they gave it the ultimate compliment: it was 'le style anglais'.

When they had finished purring over my coat, we all squeezed into the Land Rover and drove to the church in the village. From the doorway I could see that the place was packed with people all as smartly dressed as the de Lafittes. I kept close behind them, hoping it wouldn't show that I had no idea what I was meant to do. At the doorway, each of them in turn dipped their hand in a font of holy water and went down on one knee making the sign of the cross. I tried to copy Matthilde but I had a horrible feeling that I got the left and right in the wrong order.

We shuffled into a pew and each of them knelt for a while praying. I sat feeling rather uncomfortable. Neither my father or mother go to church and I know Dad doesn't approve of religion. I felt as if at any moment a finger would be pointed at me and I'd be singled out as a pagan impostor.

I'd expected a proper Roman Catholic service to be rather grand, all in Latin with loads of incense. But the service was in French and the hymns sounded more like folk songs. Towards the end of the service people started getting up from their seats and lining up in front of the altar. I got up too but Madame de Lafitte asked in a whisper if I'd been confirmed, and when I shook my head she said that I should stay where I was.

The church was even older than Les Rochers; Madame de Lafitte had told me it was twelfth century. Left alone in the pew, I had a chance to look round. The walls were covered with suffering saints and strange grimacing gargoyles, and in a niche there was a chipped and black-ened statue of the Virgin Mary.

The proper Catholics had lined up in the aisle waiting their turn to get to the altar. As each person arrived, they knelt before the priest and he bent down and placed something in their mouths and gave them a sip from a chalice. It brought back something I'd learnt at school about the body and blood of Christ. The bread was meant to be the body and the wine was the blood. Was it all just superstition? Somehow, way back, all the bible stories had got mixed in my mind with other stories, part real, part fiction – miracles and magic, angels and fairies, Saint Nicholas and Santa Claus. But superstition or not, all these people seemed to be taking it very seriously.

Matthilde returned with her mouth tight shut and knelt down in the pew to pray. I watched her bended head. *She* belonged here. No doubt she'd been chris-tened here and her parents Marie-Christine and Pierre must have got married here. I had some pretty self-righteous thoughts about the scene in the café at that point. One day Matthilde would get married in this church, like all the rest of the family. I had a sudden vision of her in a bridal veil walking down the aisle on her father's arm. And as she reached the end . . .

No! With the tedious uncontrollable way imaginations have, mine had conjured up Michel standing there. Michel! But they were cousins, I reassured myself. Yet cousins got married all the time in France. French families were really close. Suddenly all the little signs and hints added up. Of course Matthilde and Michel would get married, everyone was expecting them to.

I stared at Matthilde. She'd finished praying and was sitting up in her pew looking virtuous. I tried to picture her grown-up and married. I reckoned she'd turn out just like Marie-Christine, ready to run off with a handsome stranger the minute her husband's back was turned.

As the service came to an end, everyone linked hands in sing-along fashion. But I didn't feel like joining in. The thought of Michel and Matthilde married had sent me to the depths of gloom.

The gloom lifted somewhat when we got back to Les Rochers. The dining room table had been laid for a smart breakfast. In front of my place and Matthilde's and Michel's, there was a square box wrapped in glossy paper with a ribbon. Easter eggs – so the French had them after all.

Madame de Lafitte and Matthilde disappeared into the kitchen and after a few minutes returned with a big tray of coffee and chocolate and hot milk, a basket of hot croissants and a load of hard-boiled eggs. I was starving by now and ready to dig in. But Michel was insisting for some reason that we should open our Easter eggs first.

'Mais non,' said Matthilde. 'Après le petit déjeuner.'

A bit of an argument broke out but Michel got his way. Matthilde rolled her eyes and undid the ribbon on her box. She took the top off and then let out a scream. 'Edith!'

Chaos broke out at that point as Matthilde threw her arms around Michel's neck. Old Oncle Charles caught sight of Edith and in his short-sighted way assumed this was some rodent and started swatting at her with his table napkin. Edith made a dash for safety into the basket of croissants.

Monsieur de Lafitte was utterly furious. He got to his feet demanding that the animal was removed from the table 'tout de suite!'. After that Michel was back in the doghouse. Monsieur de Lafitte positively bristled every time he caught sight of him.

But he was back in favour with Matthilde. She totally fawned over him. I watched guardedly for signs of interest on Michel's part. But he treated Matthilde exactly the same as ever.

Chapter Twelve

During the days that followed, life seemed to fall into an easy pace. The good weather continued. Monsieur de Lafitte went back to Paris, which was a great relief. Meals were less stiff and formal and we had most of them outside. In the evening we ate on the terrace. The warm stones stored the heat of the day and in the evening they radiated it back. We never had weather as good as this in April back home.

It was great to laze around in shorts and sandals with bare legs. The house had lost its cold damp feel which was replaced by a warm smell of mown grass and beeswax. Mown grass because Michel had been roped in to mowing the lawns for Monsieur de Lafitte as a penance. It wasn't much of a penance really because the de Lafittes had a sit-on motor mower. It was an ancient thing that made a terrible noise but Michel had taken to it with a typical boy's intensity, mowing endlessly back and forth as if his life depended on it.

Matthilde was devoting herself to serious sunbathing sessions. Each morning she arranged herself on the best sunlounger with professional precision. She had to have her favourite bath sheet underneath, her tanning lotion and bottle of water to hand and an old wind-up timer from the kitchen to warn her to turn over every half hour. Once she was satisfied everything was in place, she would plug in her iPod, slip on her sunglasses, take up her book and stretch out. As the weather got hotter, Michel stripped to the waist and I couldn't help noticing he was pretty nicely tanned already. Matthilde pretended not to take any interest. But I could see her sneaking the odd look at him from behind her book.

I hadn't brought any books with me but Madame de Lafitte had found me an old French primer which she said I should study to improve my French. It had ink-black illustrations of some family called the Bruns who seemed to be on a perpetual holiday with their dog. It had little bits of story which were followed by exercises where you had to fill in the missing words. Someone had done some of the exercises before me in childish pencil handwriting and got a lot of words wrong. It was a bit like doing crosswords and after a while it became quite obsessive. I'd never been that interested in learning French before, but all of a sudden it seemed to matter.

One afternoon I was struggling with the complexities of a fishing incident, busy crossing out the words from the person before me and substituting mine, with my eyes growing sore from the brightness of the page, when

I suddenly noticed I was alone. Matthilde must have gone inside for a drink or something. I took the opportunity to stretch out on her sunlounger and closed my eyes. It was heavenly just lying there soaking in the warmth of the sun. I'd reached the ultimate point of laziness. I peered through half-closed eyes and caught sight of Michel, looking really yummy as he mowed another long straight line down the lawn. I wished the holiday could last for ever.

I must have fallen asleep because I woke after some time to find the sun had gone in. A chilly breeze had got up so I decided to go inside and change. Michel had promised to play boules with us later but he'd be ages yet, he still had the lawn on the other side of the house to mow. I gathered up my things and went back into the house wondering where Matthilde had got to.

Once changed, I went to her room to find her. As I knocked on her door I heard a distinct sound of sobbing.

'Matthilde,' I said. 'Can I come in?'

She didn't answer so I opened the door a slit. She was lying on her bed, her face was red from crying; she grabbed a handkerchief as I came in.

'What is it?' I asked, closing the door behind me.

I suddenly thought of Marie-Christine. Maybe she'd found out about her mother's affair or even worse — maybe her father had. No doubt it had all blown up into a typically French emotional drama.

'Eez nothing,' she said, blowing her nose.

'Yes it is. You can tell me,' I said. 'I think I know already.'

''Ee 'as a girlfriend,' she said with a snuffle.

This threw me into total confusion. 'Who?'

'Michel!'

It was my turn to be upset now. But I wasn't going to let Matthilde see. Anyway I wanted proof.

'How do you know?' I demanded.

She got up and checked through the window that Michel was still busy mowing.

'I show you,' she said, beckoning me to follow her.

She led me up the winding turret staircase to the upper floor where Michel's room was. She opened the door quietly. Inside was the usual scene of boy chaos: discarded socks and muddy trainers, CDs and film magazines all over the place and his guitar propped up on his unmade bed.

'See,' said Matthilde, pointing at the mirror. In the corner, slipped in between the mirror and the frame, was a photo of a blonde girl. It was an arty black and white shot. She was really pretty from what you could see, her hair was blowing across her face. In the corner it was signed 'Caroline' with a cross for a kiss.

Caroline! That was what Charlie always called me. I stared at the photo, I supposed she did look a bit like me. I mean tons better looking and much older, but she was the same blonde fair-skinned type. She looked at least seventeen or eighteen.

'Who is she?' I whispered to Matthilde.

'I don't know,' she whispered back.

Suddenly it all made sense. The way Michel kept disappearing like that; he had a girlfriend, a secret girlfriend, maybe someone his grandparents wouldn't approve of.

The two of us stared despondently at the picture of this older woman. Typical, I thought, boys of sixteen always went for older girls.

Matthilde pulled at my sleeve. 'We go,' she said.

I noticed that the lawnmower had stopped and a glance out of the window showed it abandoned at the end of the lawn. We heard footsteps in the house below. We got down the winding staircase just in time to miss Michel as he came up the main staircase two at a time.

So Michel had a girlfriend. I locked myself in the bathroom while I recovered from this news. I stared at my reflection in the bathroom mirror, feeling really young and stupid. Of course that kiss had been a mistake. What I'd built up into a great big thing in my mind was nothing. Or even worse, he'd probably thought I'd done it on purpose and was laughing at me. It was obvious that someone as gorgeous as Michel would go for an older girl. I felt utterly wretched. I vowed from now on not to take the least bit of notice of him. I'd had enough of being humiliated. There wasn't long to go before the end of the holiday. It shouldn't be too hard to stay out of his way.

After I'd washed my face and dabbed some make-up on I went downstairs. Michel was outside setting out the boules ready for a game on the gravel. Matthilde was sitting on the fence swinging her legs watching him. She'd put some make-up on too, in fact quite a lot. She didn't look a bit as if she'd been crying. In fact, she was making a big show of being her totally normal nonchalant self.

' 'Annah, come and play,' Michel called out.

'No, it's OK. You two play. I've got my book,' I called back, waving it at them. Matthilde shrugged and climbed down from the fence and Michel gave me a puzzled look.

I settled down on the sunlounger and opened my book. The Bruns had their fishing lines in the water and the dog was stealing something from their picnic basket. Between lines of this riveting story, I could hear Michel and Matthilde alternately laughing and arguing over the score while the boules landed with a heavy thunk and chink on the gravel. I would've loved to join in actually but I went and helped Madame de Lafitte instead. I laid the table on the terrace before she even asked. The others arrived just as I was finishing. Matthilde raised her eyebrows and Michel made a sign in the air like a halo over his head to indicate how virtuous I was.

I didn't eat much at dinner. Madame de Lafitte was saying something about the weekend. It seemed there was going to be some sort of party in the barn. It was an annual affair with a barbecue and over a hundred people were invited. All the young people from round about would be coming.

All the young people? My heart missed a beat and caught up with a sickening thud. I had a fleeting vision of this Caroline, the one from the photo, appearing through the crowd. If she was local, she was bound to be asked. And she must be local, otherwise how would Oncle Charles know about her?

I glanced over at Matthilde. She hadn't caught the significance of this and was asking her grandmother whether various friends had been remembered. I listened with half an ear as all the Sabines and Laurences and Thierrys and Antoines were listed. There was a big groan as Arnaud's name came up. They were all French, I thought despondently. I'd get totally left out. I could picture myself now sitting there and watching while Caroline sat with her hair flopping into her eyes in that oh-so-seductive French way *making up to Michel*.

Later that evening I was making my way crossly upstairs to my room when I met Michel coming down.

'Rosbif?' he whispered.

'Yes?'

He cast a glance over the banisters to see if anyone was around. 'You want watch another of Charlie's movies tonight?' he asked.

For a moment I was tempted. But I knew I was only tormenting myself. Michel had a girlfriend. I should stay well clear.

I shook my head. 'Non, je suis trop fatiguée,' I said with dignity.

'Too tired?' he asked. I mean he must've noticed I'd hardly budged from the sunlounger all day.

'Oui,' I said and continued on my way.

I didn't go straight to bed. I sat in a chair by the window. Madame de Lafitte's primer was on the table. I only had a few pages to go before I finished it. I turned to the end, which had a picture of the Bruns' dog stealing a string of sausages. All of a sudden it all looked childish and silly. What was the point of learning French anyway?

I was just about to go to bed when I heard footsteps on the gravel below. There was a muffled laugh and I recognised Matthilde's and then Michel's voice. They continued on their way to the terrace and I heard the French windows click shut. Maybe Matthilde was going to be treated to one of Charlie's movies tonight. This thought brought a wave of misery. Why oh why had I turned him down?

But Michel had a girlfriend, I reminded myself. Knowing Matthilde, she wouldn't care. She'd just consider her fair competition. The sound of her laugh came back to me. It had gained significance in the interval. Now it wasn't just a laugh, it was a joke against me. In fact, it was evidence of everything that had been going on behind my back.

I lay in bed that night having some deep philosophical thoughts about boys.

1) You meet someone absolutely gorgeous and you're in your seventh heaven.

2) Only trouble is, every other girl thinks he's gorgeous too.

3) He starts giving you attention and you simply can't believe it!

4) You shouldn't. He's doing the same to all the other girls.

5) With dignity you back off.

6) Which gives the others the chance to move in!

Ugggghhhhrrrr!

Chapter Thirteen

I slept badly that night, convinced as I was that Matthilde and Michel were having the time of their lives without me. I came downstairs preparing myself to face them, trying to put on a suitably dignified expression.

Matthilde was at the breakfast table, Michel was nowhere to be seen. By the look of her, she'd slept as badly as I had. Or maybe she'd been up half the night – *watching vintage movies.*

'Bonjour, 'Annah,' she said between spoonfuls of yogurt.

I grunted a kind of mumbled 'hi' and reached for a slice of bread.

Matthilde licked her spoon and looked at me thoughtfully. 'You are not 'appy, no?'

'I'm fine,' I said.

'I sink we go back to Paris,' she said abruptly.

I stopped chewing mid-mouthful and stared at Matthilde. Come to think of it, she didn't look particularly pleased with herself. Maybe I'd been jumping to conclusions. A nasty little wave of relief passed through me.

'Yes,' I said. 'Maybe we should.'

'J'appelle Maman,' she said, reaching for her mobile.

I watched as she dialled up the number.

I heard her mother answer.

'She eez in zee car – on the autoroute back to Paris,' whispered Matthilde.

I nodded. They continued talking back and forth for ages, too fast to make out what Matthilde was saying.

'Eez OK. They should be back by eighteen hours,' she said as she rang off.

'They?' My suspicions came back tenfold. 'Who was she with?'

Matthilde shrugged. 'She no say.'

'So *can* we go back?'

'Oui. Demain,' she replied.

I finished my breakfast, trying to come to terms with this turn of events. Half of me was glad we were leaving. There wasn't much point in staying. But clearly nothing had gone on last night between Michel and Matthilde. Perhaps there was still the tiniest chink of hope for me.

I spent the day revisiting my favourite haunts. The orchard where I'd been pelted by tiny apples that first morning. The steps down to the moat where Michel and I had sat and I'd tried to teach him to say the 'H' of Hannah. The pantry where we'd made strawberry baguettes. The staircase we'd crept up in the dark, trying not to make the stairs creak. I paused at the little piece of parquet outside my bedroom door. A thrill of pleasure ran through my body as I remembered that moment. This was where Michel either had or hadn't kissed me.

As I stood there, I heard a car draw up. I went to the window and saw Monsieur de Lafitte stride into the house carrying his briefcase. Curses. I wanted to make the most of our last evening, now he was going to spoil it all.

Dinner was a miserable meal. Madame de Lafitte kept going on about Matthilde's sudden announcement that we were going back to Paris. She wanted to know why and I could see Matthilde trying to make up excuses that didn't quite convince her grandmother.

'And you will miss the soirée on samedi,' Madame de Lafitte said, appealing to me for help.

Monsieur de Lafitte seemed equally put out. All through the meal he kept making pointed remarks about our departure, saying to me, 'Of course if you prefer Paris to ze country . . .'

Michel was quiet and unresponsive. Old Oncle Charles kept trying to make Matthilde change her mind.

After dinner we had coffee on the terrace. It was a hot sultry night and dark clouds were massing overhead. The air felt damp and heavy and I noticed the swallows were flying low. They swept in over the terrace, filling it with their whistling cries. Old Oncle Charles got to his feet and walked to the edge of the lawn and looked hard at the sky. He said something about 'un orage'.

'What's that?' I asked.

'A storm. What a pity. And eez your last night,' said Madame de Lafitte with a sigh.

Far in the distance I caught the first faint rumble of thunder. Madame de Lafitte started clearing the coffee things and Michel was sent upstairs to close all the windows.

I lingered on the terrace. There were no stars that night and the sky seemed to hang low over the landscape. I was just about to go in when Michel shot through the door and started walking fast and angrily across the lawn.

'Hi,' I said.

He didn't reply.

I went after him. 'Michel?'

'What?' he asked. I could tell from his voice that he was trying not to cry.

'What is it?'

'I am coming to Paris with you tomorrow,' he said briefly.

'Oh?' I said, my heart lifting in spite of his mood.

'My father and grandfather say I must go back, prepare for school. I 'ave to sign for the classics course.'

'I see,' I said, biting my lip.

He hesitated as if about to say something and then thought better of it. 'So . . . I must go pack.'

I nodded. 'I've packed already.'

I watched as he turned and walked despondently back into the house.

I went and sat on the sunlounger by the moat after that. I could see the light on in Michel's room and his shadow was cast long across the lawn as he went back and forth collecting up his things. You wouldn't have thought that even a shadow could look miserable.

Matthilde came out after a while and sat beside me on the sunlounger.

'Michel is coming with us,' I said.

She nodded. 'I know. 'Ee eez not very 'appy.'

We both looked up at his window. As we did so, lightning flashed across the garden. Somehow the weather seemed to match our mood. It felt tense and edgy. Another flash of lightning lit the clouds up in hard relief. The sound of the thunder grew louder and more threatening.

Then, with a suddenness that took my breath away, the wind got up. It came like a blast from an opened door, tearing through the trees, scattering torn leaves and broken twigs in its path. My hair was blowing in my eyes and my clothes were glued to my body by the force of it.

'Ça y est,' said Matthilde and got to her feet.

Within minutes we were grabbing at deckchairs as the wind tried to rip them from our grasp. We ran half stumbling, dragging as much as we could, in the direction of the barn. The rain came pelting down in mammoth drops. We forced our way against it, scattering books and towels. By the time we got into the barn, it was positively deluging. We struggled back through the rain into the house, breathless and half-soaked.

When I tried the kitchen light switch, nothing happened. The storm must have knocked the electricity out. Matthilde started pulling out drawers, looking for candles.

Between the rolls of thunder the house was eerily silent. Everyone else seemed to have gone to bed. After one particularly heavy clap of thunder, I heard a miserable whine and found the dogs cowering under the table. Madame de Lafitte must have allowed them inside because of the storm. Titan was shaking all over and Sultan was crouched on the ground gnawing obsessively at something.

Matthilde knelt down and put her arms around Titan and then said, 'Dis donc, Sultan a mangé les cartes.' The wrecked pack of cards was spread around him in chewed fragments.

There were footsteps in the hall and by the light of another lightning flash I saw Michel standing in the doorway. His hair was all ruffed up and he looked wretched.

'It is too early to sleep,' he said.

Matthilde pointed at the wrecked pack, indicating that a game of cards was out of the question. I could tell they were discussing what to do when Matthilde suggested a game called cache-cache.

'What's that?' I asked.

Matthilde tried to explain and I said without thinking, 'Sounds like sardines.'

'Sardines? What is that?' asked Michel.

'Is a fish,' said Matthilde.

When I told them the rules, Matthilde's eyes gleamed mischievously. I suddenly realised what she was up to. This was her last chance. I had a fleeting vision of her squeezed into a cupboard with Michel. Or maybe it would be me squeezed in with him. What if he thought I'd suggested the game on purpose? It would be *so embarrassing*.

'But it's a kid's game,' I backtracked. 'Pour enfants. Very childish.'

Another flash of lightning lit the room like strobe-light. Through the open doorway I caught a glimpse of the boar's glass eyes glinting in the hall. I shivered.

'You are scared?' asked Matthilde. I could hear the scorn in her voice.

'No, of course not,' I lied. 'But your grandparents, they wouldn't like it.'

Michel put a finger to his lips. 'Then we must be ve-ry silencieux.'

'So – we play?' said Matthilde.

I nodded reluctantly. I watched as Michel tossed for who was going to hide. First I was eliminated, next Matthilde, so it was him.

'A bientôt, mes filles,' he said with a wicked grin and crept out of the room.

I started counting to a hundred with a pounding

heart. Matthilde was counting too but in French. She finished first, which was kind of odd when you consider how long it takes to say things like 'quatre-vingt-dix-sept'.

She made her way out through the kitchen door before I'd even got to eighty-two. She was nowhere to be seen by the time I reached the hall.

As I did so the lightning sent a ragged flash through the hallway and thunder crashed overhead. I hesitated for a moment, considering. There were far more places to hide upstairs. Especially in the rooms they didn't use. Another shiver ran down my spine as I thought of what might be hidden in them. But I pulled myself together with determination and started to tiptoe up the dark staircase.

Once at the top, I paused again and listened. There was not a sound to indicate anyone was alive. To the left were the bedrooms occupied by Monsieur and Madame de Lafitte and old Oncle Charles – so out of bounds. To the right were the unused bedrooms with the furniture draped spookily in dustsheets. Steeling myself, I selected one of these and slid open the door.

Lightning flashed again and it was as much as I could do to stop myself racing down the stairs to cower under the table with the dogs. But the thought of Matthilde's scorn gave me courage. I gritted my teeth and started feeling my way from one piece of furniture to another.

I nearly jumped out of my skin as another flash of lightning outlined a coatstand which looked eerily like a person. Darkness engulfed the room once more and I bumped into some piece of furniture and froze. The hair on the back of my neck was rising in panic and little prickles of goose-pimples were running down my arms. Still silence. I listened intently for the slightest movement in the darkness. Breathing even. And then the thunder boomed overhead so loudly it seemed to shake the house.

My hand touched something that felt *like an arm*! I pulled back the dustsheet. Only an armchair. Empty. I listened again. Where could Matthilde have got to? And Michel? Maybe she'd found him already. Maybe they were hidden together, right now. This thought made me continue. I'd try another room.

The neighbouring room was even darker. I waited for another flash of lightning. Tense minutes ticked by. And then it came. Lighting up a four-poster bed with the curtains drawn round. I was sure it hadn't been like that when I last saw it. I forced myself to feel inside. Emptiness, silence, nothing. I was starting to feel desperate. Matthilde might be searching downstairs. Maybe Michel had never come up. It was as if the two of them had totally dematerialised.

I stood stock-still in the inky darkness, every nerve in my body on red alert for the slightest sound. Nothing moved. I fumbled my way back to the doorway meaning to try downstairs. But I'd forgotten a chaise-longue draped in a dustsheet. As I stumbled into it, a hand came out of nowhere and grabbed me by the wrist. I stifled a scream as a voice whispered, 'H-annah, c'est moi.

'Vite,' Michel said, pulling me under with him. He shook the dustsheet back over us. I could feel the warmth of him very close. I curled myself up as small as possible on the far side of the chaise-longue and tried to stop my heart thudding in my chest. Rival emotions had set up a battle inside me. Hope and despair in equal proportions. I told myself firmly, he had a girlfriend – whatever happened, I was going to be totally cool with him. But my skin prickled with anticipation all the same.

I felt his hand, warm and familiar, reaching for mine. He pulled me towards him. I was absolutely positive he was going to kiss me again – properly this time. But I wasn't going to let him. I had my pride.

I was just pulling away when we heard the door creak open and more footsteps in the room. We both froze. Feet were making their way across the carpet. There was a creak as a cupboard door was opened and closed. Matthilde wasn't being nearly so careful to be quiet. She was positively lumbering around. It was at that point that I felt a terrible urge to sneeze. I tried to hold it back, but it didn't really matter since she'd lost the game anyway. As I sneezed, the dustsheet was whipped off us. I looked up and to my horror saw it wasn't Matthilde at all. It was Monsieur de Lafitte standing there. He was holding a walking stick threateningly in one hand and in the other he had Titan by the collar.

'Qu'est que vous faites?' he demanded angrily.

Michel leaped to his feet and I climbed out of the chaise-longue and stood beside him blushing to the roots of my hair.

Michel was trying to explain about the game but Monsieur de Lafitte wasn't listening. Matthilde appeared in the doorway and tried to calm him down. But Monsieur de Lafitte kept going on about 'cambrioleurs'. I'd never heard the word 'cambrioleur' before. It sounded like someone horribly loose and immoral. He was absolutely livid with both of us.

He turned to me. ''Annah, you go to bed *now*,' he said.

'Oui, monsieur,' I said. I crept past and made my way as fast as I could to my room.

It was impossible to sleep that night. It was ironic really. I'd been going on and on about how free and easy the French were with their love lives. And now I was being labelled a loose English girl. Unjustly, as it happened.

As the night progressed the thunder rolled away but the rain continued deluging the house. I lay there listening to it pounding on the roof above. The wind howled through the attic and the house creaked as if it were a massive ship in a storm at sea.

Chapter Fourteen

The next day I got dressed dreading what would happen when I went downstairs. I was packed and ready to go. I couldn't wait to be on that train to Paris.

But I came down to find my 'shocking behaviour' of the night before had sunk into insignificance. The whole place was in chaos.

There were muddy boot prints all over the hallway and the front doors were standing open in spite of a cold wind. I went to look out. The rain was still coming down in sheets and through the deluge I saw what all the fuss was about. The river had burst its banks and the moat had disappeared from sight. It had turned into a kind of lake which was spreading up the lawn towards the house. I strained my eyes down the avenue of trees. The road had totally disappeared under water. It had turned into a river. I could see water rushing through the stunted trees in an angry current, carrying branches and bits of fence along with it. There was no way we could get down it to catch the train.

In the distance, I spotted Monsieur de Lafitte in waders trying to guide a man in a mechanical digger down the bank. Madame de Lafitte came hurrying through the hall wearing an outsized raincoat. 'Oh, 'Annah. Quel désastre, le jardin, mes roses.'

I followed her gaze. The tips of the rosebushes we had pruned just a week or so ago were fast disappearing under the eddying water. At the high-water mark, I caught sight of the figure of old Oncle Charles. He stood leaning on his stick as if defying the water to rise any further.

Madame de Lafitte went and joined him and I heard him say something in a serious voice to her about 'le pont'. Matthilde came down the stairs behind me and stood aghast, staring at the flood.

'We can't leave,' I said.

'Non,' she agreed and then she exclaimed something that sounded like: 'Regarde le pont.'

'What is "le pont"?' I asked.

'Le pont. The bridge,' she said. 'Oh mon dieu.'

I could barely see the bridge. It was submerged up to its arch in the swirling water. It was in centre stream, taking the full force of the current. Already one of the massive stones had broken loose, leaving an ugly gap like a missing tooth. Surely this bridge, which had stood for centuries, couldn't be swept away just like that?

Matthilde and I got kitted out in raincoats and gumboots and went to see what we could do to help. Michel was out there already, driving Monsieur de Lafitte's tractor mower with a trailer attached. He was carting stuff down the bank.

People had come up from the surrounding farms to help. Monsieur de Lafitte had organised them into a sort of chain gang and they were passing sandbags from hand to hand. Matthilde and I were given the job of filling sandbags. A big mound of sand had been dumped in front of the barn and there was a pile of sacks beside it. Matthilde held the bags open while I shovelled the sand in. Narcisse then tied them tight with string and humped them into the trailer. Once full Michel drove the trailer down to the bank and the first man in the chain lugged them out.

It was wet and dirty work and my hands soon felt horribly sore from the rough sand. There was panic in the air, with shouts coming from all directions as more leaks appeared along the bank. Everyone was working flat out to stem the flow. But despite all our efforts, I could see the water inexorably rising.

Damp sand is heavy stuff and after thirty bags or so I was out of breath and slowing down. Matthilde reached out and took the spade from me, indicating that we should change places. She had rain running down her face and great splashes of mud up her arms, but for once she didn't seem to care, she worked with silent determination, her teeth gritted.

The rain continued to pour down and I could see Madame de Lafitte trying to persuade old Oncle Charles to go inside. But he stood there defiantly, as if made of stone, with the rain dripping off his hat and running down his neck.

Each time Michel came back with the trailer he gave us a wink or a grin. Matthilde looked up and caught his eye and I could see that for once she got an admiring glance. Gradually, the barrage we were building against the flood piled up. But however many sandbags we filled, the river seemed to find a new way round and the torrent rose as fast as ever.

Monsieur de Lafitte came up to us eventually and signalled to us to stop. I stood stretching my aching back, surveying the scene of disaster. Matthilde went and joined old Oncle Charles and I saw, under her persuasion, he allowed himself to be led back to the house.

Some of the men had gathered in a little knot upstream from the bridge. They were leaning over what looked like a winch of some sort. Michel and I went to see what the men were trying to do. We watched as one of them lowered a chain with a hook on the end into the water. Each time he did so, the force of the current carried the chain downstream and he had to drag it back and try again.

'What's he doing?' I asked.

'Eez the water gate,' said Michel. 'They want to raise it, but the cable eet is broken.'

I stared down. Sure enough, like everything else at Les Rochers, the cable had been allowed to rust away. The gate itself was submerged way below the water level. Judging by the length of the chain it was several metres down. The men were trying unsuccessfully to latch on to it with the hook.

'Why doesn't someone go down with it?' I asked.

Michel shrugged. 'The space is too small for a man to pass.'

I looked down. It was true, the floodgate was at the end of a sort of gully. Over the years it had got choked with mud and stones.

'But I could swim down,' I said.

Monsieur de Lafitte looked up at that point and said something that sounded like 'trop dangereux'.

'But I'm a really strong swimmer,' I protested.

Michel nodded. 'Oui. C'est vrai.'

Monsieur de Lafitte looked at me assessingly. The man with the hook paused as he explained in French what I was suggesting. One of the men held out a rope, indicating that he could make a sort of safety harness.

Monsieur de Lafitte turned back to me. ' 'Annah, tu es sûre? You want to do this?'

'Oui,' I said with determination.

'Very well,' he said. 'We try.'

I went up to my room to change with a beating heart. It wasn't far to swim down. An absolute cinch in a swimming pool. I'd done the same thing over and over again in the school pool, diving for coins. But the water in the gully was opaque with mud and you couldn't tell what was down there.

I dragged on my swimsuit with shaking hands, trying to get the better of my imagination. Encounters with eels and getting trapped in tangling weed were the least of it. Pulling my mac on over my swimsuit I hurried back to the disaster scene.

By the time I rejoined the group, one of the men had fashioned the ropes into a sort of harness for me. They were strong nylon ropes and he tugged hard at them to make sure they would hold.

Monsieur de Lafitte fixed the harness around me with a serious face. There was dead silence as I bent to lower myself over the side. There was only one way to go down – head first. I took the hook in my hand and as I did so looked up and caught Michel's eye. He looked tense and anxious but he smiled encouragingly as I bent forward to take the plunge.

Suddenly, I was engulfed in icy water. When I opened my eyes, I couldn't see a thing, but I swam down as hard and fast as I could. One, two, three, four strokes. I groped down the wall feeling for the gate in the dark water. I'd just caught at it with the tips of my fingers when I felt a tug on the rope. All of a sudden I was being pulled up to the surface. I broke through the water and took a deep breath. A semicircle of anxious faces was staring down at me.

'Trop tôt,' I said. Which means too soon.

I estimated that I had to swim just one stroke deeper and then I would be level with the gate.

'Encore?' asked Monsieur de Lafitte.

I nodded. I swam down strongly, counting the strokes this time. One, two, three, four, five strokes. My fingers latched on to the gate. I could feel the metal ring at the top where the cable had been attached. But the chain coming down from above had got twisted somehow and the hook wouldn't reach. With the last of my strength I gave it the most tremendous tug and it came loose. I felt the hook slide into the ring just as a pull on my harness hauled me up to the surface once more.

The faces looked even more anxious this time. Gasping for breath, I said, 'I think I did it!'

Monsieur de Lafitte tested the chain.

'Ça y est!' he roared. Michel leaned down and pulled me out of the water and Madame de Lafitte rushed forward and wrapped a towel around me.

We stood aside as the men lined up to haul on the chain like a tug-of-war. At the first attempt nothing happened. They took a breath and heaved again. There was a grinding sound and they tottered back a few steps. This was followed by a tremendous gurgling and gushing below. A great sloosh of water leaped out on the far side of the moat with the force of Niagara. There was a lot of slapping on backs and incomprehensible French comments as we watched with a kind of awe as the water flooded out in a torrent on to the water meadows beyond. It was as if a giant plug had been taken out of a bath.

One of the fellows went up to the high-water mark and shoved a stick into the ground. At first it didn't seem to make any difference. But then the tidemark started shrinking inch by inch down the lawn.

All at once they all broke into a cheer. Monsieur de Lafitte turned to me and lifted me up into the air in a huge hug.

'La petite anglaise!' he shouted.

Everyone wanted to hug and kiss me. I had so many mwah-mwahs from rough unshaven burly farmers, it felt as if my skin was being flayed. I found I was shaking from cold. Florence had appeared in the kitchen doorway calling out something about lunch and everyone turned in a kind of muddy procession back to the house. As soon as we were inside, Madame de Lafitte bundled me upstairs for a hot bath.

I lay in the bath trying to get over the shivery sensation which I think was more from nerves than the cold. I kept on having flashbacks of what might have happened if the rope had got caught or there had been something really nasty down there.

There was a knock on the bathroom door.

''Annah, you OK?'

It was Matthilde.

'Can I come in?'

I climbed out of the bath, wrapped myself in a towel and let her in.

She was carrying a big glass of hot milk.

'Grandpère say you must drink zis.'

I took a sip and it made me catch my breath, but I felt a warmness rushing through me. Matthilde said it was hot milk with a spoonful of cognac and sugar in it.

'You were ve-ry brave,' she said. 'I could ne-ver do zat.'

'I was the only one skinny enough,' I said.

She shook her head. 'No. I would be too scared.'

'Has it stopped raining?'

She nodded and went and pulled the curtain back from the window. The flood had cleared the rosebushes and the lawn was reappearing rimmed by a ragged line of debris. Best of all, I could see the arch of the bridge was now well clear of the water. It stood looking war-torn and damaged but you could see the worst was over.

I was still feeling shaky after my bath. Madame de Lafitte brought me up a bowl of hot soup and insisted I should have a lie-down to recover. I got into bed and pulled over the covers. Normally I can't sleep during the day but the minute my head touched the pillow I instantly dropped off.

Chapter Fifteen

I woke at about four in the afternoon, feeling thick-headed and muggy, and checked outside to find the garden swarming with people. It was like the aftermath of a major disaster. Scaffolding had been erected round the bridge and some men were hard at work screwing a metal bar in place to reinforce it. There was a team of helpers in the garden raking the debris into piles to be burned.

I went down to the kitchen to find Florence lording it over a load of women who were washing salad and scrubbing potatoes and stringing meat on skewers. I wondered what was going on, so I tried one of France's more painfully convoluted phrases on her: 'Qu'est-ce qu'il se passe?'

Florence paused from her salad washing and nodded towards the barn.

'Mais c'est la fête. Ce soir.'

La fête? The party! In all the drama of the flood, I'd completely forgotten about it. Outside, a group of men was busy building a huge barbecue out of bricks and iron grilles. I could see through the barn doors that a load of trestle tables and benches had been set up in readiness.

Florence bustled past me and picked up a tray with a bowl of soup and some bread and cheese on it.

'Pauvre Monsieur Charles,' she said, shaking her head.

The baker arrived at the door at that point, weighed down by long brown paper bags bulging with enough baguettes to withstand a siege. Florence called out to him 'J'arrive' and handed me the tray, saying something which I interpreted as – would I take it up to him.

I knew where Oncle Charles's rooms were. I'd seen him going in and out of them and I'd often heard music or the sound of a television coming from inside. I carried the tray up the stairs and knocked on his door but there was no answer. When I opened it a chink, I found he was asleep wrapped in a rug in a big armchair in front of the television.

I paused in the doorway uncertain whether to wake him. His room was a kind of shrine to vintage Hollywood. A film poster yellowed with age was pinned to the wooden panelling. There were signed photos of stars where you would have expected respectable hunting prints and stiff photos of relatives. The bookshelves sagged with tattered magazines and film yearbooks. And in pride of place on the mantelpiece was a framed black and white photo of a skinny Apache on a palomino horse, which I recognised with some difficulty as a far, far younger Oncle Charles.

I went over and took the remote control and put the TV on 'hold'. This made him wake with a grunt. 'Caroline,' he exclaimed. 'Where have you been? I haven't seen you for days.'

I was sitting next to him the night before as a matter of fact, but I thought it kinder not to mention that. 'I've been helping in the garden. Because of the flood.'

'The flood?' he asked, looking confused. 'Oh, the inondation,' he said, coming to his senses. 'This house has stood here for centuries,' he continued. 'The water it rises and it falls. People come. People go. The house will be here long after we have all gone.'

I put down the tray, wondering if I should leave him to eat in peace, when he said, 'Stay a while. Keep me company?' He patted the chair beside him.

I wanted to go outside and see if I could find Michel in actual fact. It would be my last chance to see him alone.

'I'll stay for a while,' I said.

He nodded towards the television. 'You should take a look at this. *This* is the finest film ever made.'

He clicked the video on to 'play'. The film was about some man called Charlie who owned a newspaper. We watched as Charlie's empire grew and thrived, then slowly declined and he got older and balder and sadder. It wasn't the kind of movie I'd ever choose to watch but it got to me somehow. Old Oncle Charles nodded off after he'd finished his soup and I stared at him wondering whether maybe this was why he called himself Charlie. His family had once had an empire — all those farms and land and now they'd dwindled away to just the house and the park.

When the film ended, he woke up with a start and said he was going to turn in. He wasn't going to bother with the soirée, that was for the young people. I promised to come up and see him in the morning before I left.

I dumped the tray in the kitchen and went out to check how the barbecue was coming on. A satisfying glow was already coming from the red-hot charcoal. The men had fixed a whole lamb on the spit. Big difference from barbecues back home — boozy dads standing over uncontrollable fires that either billowed smoke or raged with flame and could never cook as much as a chipolata right through.

We'd been told not to dress up for the barbecue. Which was just as well since I'd got down to my very last clean clothes. I had a khaki shirt Mum had bought which I didn't like much and my jeans which unfortunately had been ironed with creases in them by Florence. But I washed my hair and took some trouble blow-drying it.

I was blow-drying my fringe which had chosen tonight to be particularly flat and difficult when I remembered the mysterious Caroline. Was she getting ready right now, staring in the mirror, blow-drying *her* hair? I jolly well hoped it rained on her and it went frizzy.

As I turned off the dryer, I caught the sound of instruments tuning up. I went down to investigate. A man with an accordion, a girl with a violin and a bearded man with a drum kit were setting up in a corner of the barn. Michel was standing talking to them, holding his guitar. He played a few chords and the man with the drums nodded and did a roll. While I watched they broke into a number. It was a song I'd heard Michel sing to himself in his room. It sent a shiver down my spine as I remembered his shadow, so close to me, on the wall.

Madame de Lafitte was calling me from the kitchen. More hands were needed to carry dishes out to the tables. I joined the team, ferrying out bowls of vegetables which had been turned, in that magical French way, into 'carottes rapées', 'céleri rémoulade' and 'ratatouille'.

It was on one of my return trips that I bumped into Matthilde. I actually did a double take. I don't know whether she hadn't heard, or was just ignoring the dress code. But if this was 'casual' I'd got it wrong. She was wearing the tightest pair of cropped jeans with really high heels. She'd topped this with an off-the shoulder T-shirt and she'd put on tons of eyeliner.

Madame de Lafitte took one look at her and her jaw dropped.

'Matthilde, ma chérie,' she started.

Matthilde gave her grandmother one of her sweetest looks. 'Oui, Grandmère?'

A look of confusion passed across Madame de Lafitte's face as she struggled to be modern and open-minded.

'Rien, ma pouce. Aide 'Annah.'

'Oui, Grandmère,' said Matthilde, as if 'beurre' wouldn't melt in her mouth. She picked up a big dish of potato salad and made for the barn. I followed, feeling really daggy. I mean, Matthilde looked as if she'd dressed for a nightclub while I had on a dreary khaki shirt which was my least favourite item of clothing.

Matthilde went the long way round with the salad, which meant she had to pass the musicians. The fellow with the drums noticed her and raised his eyebrows. I saw Michel look up and look again and then return to his guitar. I bet he thought she looked fantastic.

We were just arranging the last dishes on the table when I heard a car draw up. The first people to arrive were a family from the village. They stood around looking shy and embarrassed until Monsieur de Lafitte went up to them with a tray of drinks. But soon more and more people were flooding into the barn. Monsieur de Lafitte seemed to know everyone and this evening he didn't seem grand or stand-offish at all. In fact, he was having a good laugh with some of the men.

As people arrived I scrutinised each girl to see if she might be Caroline. There were loads of girls of about the right age. Few of them blonde enough, but maybe the blonde was dyed and she'd gone back to her natural colour. Or dyed her hair jet-black or something. I sent a searching look to Michel every time a girl came through the door. But he played on with the rest of the band, not seeming to give any one of them an interested glance.

Arnaud arrived and stood in the doorway, looking awkward. An unfortunate choice of position with his back to the barbecue. His ears glowed in the darkness like rear brake lights. I could see him casting anxious glances in Matthilde's direction. But either she hadn't seen him or she was ignoring him on purpose; she seemed intent on talking to some boys I hadn't seen before.

Eventually, the smell of roasted meat came wafting deliciously from the barbecue outside and people started taking their places at the tables. I was just about to sit down with the younger people when Monsieur de Lafitte came up to me and took me by the hand and led me to the place of honour beside him.

The tables had been set out in a long row. Most of the young people were sitting at the far end. A load of boys were shoving down their bench to allow someone in. It was Matthilde. I watched as she squeezed in between two of the bigger boys, wondering why she'd chosen to sit so far away from the rest of the family.

Michel stayed with the musicians. It seemed they were going to play while we ate and have their meal later. Plates of salads and charcuterie were soon being passed around and all the glasses were refilled, but nobody took the tiniest sip or nibble of their meal. Monsieur de

Lafitte got to his feet. Haltingly, the barn fell into a respectful silence.

He started on a very long speech in which the word 'inondation' cropped up quite a few times. I switched off while he was talking and did a person-by-person scrutiny of every female round the room. Not one of them looked anything like the photo of Caroline. I glanced over at Michel. He didn't look too cut up. In fact, he was staring in the direction of Matthilde. And then I saw why.

Matthilde was flirting unashamedly with the boy next to her. She was whispering in his ear and allowing him to whisper back really close. Luckily, Monsieur de Lafitte couldn't see what was going on. He was coming to what seemed like a climax when I heard my name followed by him raising his glass and saying, 'Bravo, la petite anglaise!'

To my horror, I was hauled to my feet as everyone raised their glasses to me and went into a round of applause. There followed an expectant silence. It seemed that I was meant to say something. I found myself standing there, going redder and redder, absolutely tongue-tied.

A hoarse whisper came from Monsieur de Lafitte: 'Merci et bon appétit.'

'Merci. Et bon appétit,' I managed to stutter.

Few phrases could have met with such enthusiasm. The applause was deafening and then everyone set to eating and drinking with the maximum noise and laughter.

'Merci,' I said to Monsieur de Lafitte as, thankfully, the attention went off me.

He looked down at me, his eyebrows bristling alarmingly.

'I mean merci, monsieur,' I corrected myself.

He raised an eyebrow at that and I saw a smile twitch at the corners of his mouth.

'Merci, mademoiselle,' he said, raising his glass to me. 'So tomorrow you leave us? Tell me, what impression you take home of France?'

I paused, wondering how to answer this. 'It surprised me.'

'Surprised you, why?'

'Well, I didn't really want to come,' I admitted.

'No? And why was zat?'

I could feel myself going hot and bothered under his gaze. I stupidly blurted out, 'Because French people seem to think they're so superior.'

Monsieur de Lafitte's eyebrows rose almost to his hairline, they positively stood on end. Then he threw back his head and roared with laughter. 'But that's because we *are* superior!' he said.

I suddenly realised where I'd gone wrong. I'd taken all his serious gazes and fierce comments to heart, when I should have stood my ground and answered back.

Monsieur de Lafitte was sharing this joke with the people all around us. My attention went back to Michel. He'd put down his guitar and he kept sending odd looks over to Matthilde. I craned round to see what she was up to. She was chatting up the boy on the other side now. She was trying to make Michel jealous and she was being pathetically obvious about it.

But Michel wasn't the only person who had noticed. Arnaud was standing alone with a drink in his hand. He was watching Matthilde with a hopeless look on his face.

They'd switched to recorded music — traditional French stuff — and people were getting up to dance. I saw Michel force his way over to Matthilde's table with a grim look on his face. She got up to dance with him. It was my turn to suffer pangs of jealousy now. Maybe Matthilde's ploy had worked.

I heard a voice say: ''Annah, danse avec moi' It was Monsieur de Lafitte. I had no choice but to accept. Monsieur de Lafitte was much taller than me and it was a really tricky dance like a quick waltz. I made a real mess of it. Besides, I was trying to keep an eye on Michel and Matthilde. They seemed to be dancing very close.

After a couple of dances, Michel went back to the band and Matthilde returned to her seat with a look of triumph on her face. This really go to me. I didn't want to risk another dance so I escaped from the dance floor and went outside.

I made my way down to the bridge. The water had subsided almost to its usual level. The frogs were back with their evening chant as if nothing had happened. So were the swallows, they were swooping back and forth skimming the surface of the moat. In the distance I could still hear the rush of water through the floodgate.

The meadows had all but disappeared from sight under water. They were shining in the moonlight like a great sheet of beaten silver. The house seemed to float in the mist, as if cut off from the real world. It stood with its witch's-hat towers silhouetted against the sky. I remembered how I'd thought it was so horribly spooky when I arrived. Now, with the lights from the windows casting long trails of brightness over the lawn, it looked quite simply magical.

I leaned on the parapet staring down into the dark water, trying to record this moment in my mind for ever. The sound of the water rushing through the floodgate was strangely hypnotic. Suddenly, I felt the presence of someone behind me.

'Rosbif!'

I swung round to find Michel.

'Bonsoir, Grenouille.'

He leaned on the wall beside me, staring down thoughtfully.

Abruptly he said, 'H-annah. Can you keep a secret?'

'Yes. Of course.' My heart was beating in my chest. This was the point at which he was going to tell me about Caroline.

But I was wrong. Instead he said, 'I am leaving tonight.'

'Leaving?'

'Yes.'

'Where are you going?'

'To Cannes. To the festival.'

'What festival?'

'The film festival.'

'Why?'

'This is a chance. I will meet people.'

'How do you know?'

'Why not?' he said stubbornly.

'But you can't just leave without telling anyone.'

'If I tell, they will make me go back to the lycée.'

'But how will you manage for money?'

He shrugged. 'I can play my guitar. At this restaurant. The boss 'ee say 'ee will pay me.'

'But you can't live like that!'

'You don't understand. I can't go back to school.'

'Michel, please don't do this . . .'

''Annah. You won't tell?'

'But . . .'

'Please, 'Annah.'

'H-annah.'

'H-annah.'

I couldn't help smiling as he tried, as ever unsuccessfully, to say my name. He put one arm on either side of me and leaned towards me, he was smiling too.

'You won't tell, will you?'

The water swept by beneath us and once again I had that giddying freefall feeling. And for a moment I didn't care whether he had a girlfriend or not. I glanced instinctively back towards the house to see if we were being watched. And, sure enough, Matthilde had come out of the barn with one of the boys. She was staring in our direction.

I twisted myself clear.

'Matthilde is watching us.'

'Ah, Matthilde,' said Michel. He looked round and saw her with the other boy. She turned deliberately and put her arms around him and they started snogging. It was at that point that Arnaud emerged from the barn. He took one look at Matthilde and went off in the direction of his car.

Michel sighed with annoyance. ' 'Ow can she be so cruel?' he said.

I watched as Michel made his way towards the couple. Then Matthilde started gesticulating at him. They were having a row – as usual.

Later that night I lay in bed wondering if Michel would really go through with his plan.

I was going back to school. Next week I would be back in ordinary everyday life. For a moment, my head filled with the familiar sounds of school – the slam of locker doors, laughter and screams, shoes scuffing on the polished lino. And the smell of it; gym clothes and floor polish, the cabbagy whiff from the canteen, the stale-egg and formaldehyde pong from the science lab . . .

Jess and Angie would want to know about the holiday in minute detail. I could just see Angie's face when I told her I'd spent most of the time in the country. My mind was already busy fabricating a somewhat more glamorous version of my holiday, suitable for her ears.

It was really difficult to sleep that night. I kept straining my ears for sounds of movement from the floor above. I hoped Michel had thought better of his crazy plan. I should have tried harder to talk him out of it. There was going to be the most almighty row if he did leave.

Chapter Sixteen

The following morning I lay listening for sounds of Michel getting up. I couldn't hear anything. Maybe he was still asleep or perhaps he was downstairs already.

I lugged my holdall down the stairs to find I was the first in the kitchen. Florence was busy making ham baguettes and heating milk for coffee and hot chocolate. The kitchen table was laid for four. I slid into a chair and helped myself to bread. Every nerve in my body was on the alert for sounds on the stairs. I heard footsteps and looked up hopefully – but it was only Matthilde. She came dragging her suitcase behind her, looking sleepy and grumpy.

A few minutes later Monsieur de Lafitte arrived. He kissed us both and then sat down at the table.

'Où est Michel?' he asked.

Matthilde mumbled something about expecting he'd be down in a minute.

Florence filled Monsieur de Lafitte's bowl with coffee. He took a slice of bread and spread it carefully with a layer of butter. I passed him the jam. Minutes ticked by as we ate in silence. I became incredibly aware of the slightest sound, the chink of metal on china, the scrape of a knife on bread, as my ears strained for the sound of Michel's footsteps. I tried to act totally normally, but my mind was racing. What would happen if Michel *had* made off? How had he left? What kind of scene would there be?

Monsieur de Lafitte kept looking at his watch and clearing his throat.

Eventually Matthilde scraped back her chair.

'Je vais le chercher,' she said.

She hurried out of the room and I heard her running up the stairs two at a time.

I sat staring at my plate. The bread felt gooey in my mouth, I swallowed it in hard lumps. Monsieur de Lafitte got up from the table and started fiddling with his car keys. The sound jarred horribly on my nerves. After a couple of minutes Matthilde came racing down the stairs. She stood in the doorway, her eyes wide with surprise.

'Il n'est pas là,' she said.

Her grandfather said something fast in an angry voice.

Matthilde shook her head. She repeated, 'Il n'est pas là. Ni ses affaires, ni sa guitare.'

Florence stopped what she was doing and stood stock-still staring at Matthilde. I hoped no one would look at me, I could tell I was going scarlet from guilt.

Monsieur de Lafitte slammed his car keys down on the table and made for the stairs. Matthilde and I followed.

He strode up the stairs, along the corridor past my room and Matthilde's and up the little winding stone staircase that led to Michel's. The door was standing open. He went in and gazed around.

From where I was standing in the doorway, I could see that the bed was unmade and the floor was still strewn with film magazines. But his clothes had gone, his trainers too and his guitar.

Monsieur de Lafitte looked around as if searching for something — a note perhaps. His eye was caught by the photo of the blonde girl. It was still there, wedged between the glass and the frame. He took it between thumb and forefinger.

'Qui est cette fille?' he demanded.

'J'ai aucune idée,' said Matthilde with an angry frown.

Taking the photo with him, Monsieur de Lafitte made off down the stairs. We followed. Monsieur de Lafitte picked up the phone in his study and started dialling. Matthilde stood beside him listening.

The photograph lay on the hall table. I picked it up. Close up, I could see it wasn't an ordinary snapshot. And the signature in the corner wasn't just 'Caroline'. It had been partially covered by the frame of the mirror. I could now see the name 'Caroline Carr' scrawled across the photo like a star's signature beside the kiss. I turned it over. It was a publicity photo. On the back there was a list of the films she'd appeared in. All in the 1950s. I realised with a shock that if Caroline Carr was still around she'd be old enough to be Michel's *grandmother*! Rival emotions fought inside me. Relief that this wasn't his girlfriend. And confusion as to why he had the photo anyway.

I strained my ears listening to Monsieur de Lafitte's phone call. He was calling Michel's mobile. It must have been on answerphone, because he left a curt message which I didn't understand. Then he put down the receiver. He glanced at his watch and said, 'Bon, nous avons raté le train.'

We'd missed the train and apparently there wasn't another for Paris until two that afternoon, which meant there was no way I could make my flight home that day.

A perfectly horrid couple of hours followed. We all searched round for signs of Michel and soon discovered that one of the bikes had gone. Matthilde suggested he'd taken it into his head to go out for a late-night bike ride, though why he should have taken all his stuff she couldn't think.

Madame de Lafitte then went into a flat panic and phoned the police to see if there had been any accidents. There were several tense moments before they confirmed that there hadn't. Everyone was coming up with theories of where Michel had gone. And *why* he had gone. I felt really uncomfortable. I made the excuse to go to my room and ring my parents to tell them I couldn't get back that day.

Mum answered. 'Hannah, poppet. Are you on the train?'

'No. That's why I'm calling, we missed it. Which means I'm going to miss my plane too.'

Mum then started fussing about the expense. I had a ticket that couldn't be changed.

'But it's worse than that,' I interrupted her. 'Michel, Matthilde's cousin – he's disappeared.'

'Michel? He's a boy?'

'Yes.'

'You mean Phillippe's son?'

'I don't know what his father's called.'

'It must be Phillippe's son. He's a bit of a problem apparently.'

'It sounds to me as if the whole family has problems.'

'Oh yes, his mother! She's a friend of Marie-Christine. I only met her once but . . .'

I could tell that Mum was going to start on one of her big tedious reminiscence sessions, so I interrupted, 'Look, I don't know quite what's going to happen. Monsieur de Lafitte says he'll book me a new ticket. I'll ring you as soon as I know more, OK?'

Back downstairs I found Matthilde and Madame de Lafitte standing in the hall. I could hear Monsieur de Lafitte talking on the phone in his study.

''Ee eez calling my uncle. Michel's father,' whispered Matthilde.

Monsieur de Lafitte put the phone down and came to join us. I could tell the news wasn't good. Michel hadn't been in touch with his father. He had no idea where he could have gone.

At that point I heard the *tap tap tap* of old Oncle Charles's stick coming down the corridor. Monsieur and Madame de Lafitte exchanged glances and I was sent back to the hall to fetch the photo as if it was a valuable piece of evidence.

The old man took it, shaking his head sadly. He mumbled something and turned the photo over and showed the back. Monsieur de Lafitte listened with a look of impatience on his face. He'd obviously hoped it would be a lead and it wasn't.

After that everyone seemed to have a different idea of what should be done. Monsieur de Lafitte wanted to go off in the car and do a search of the surrounding roads. Matthilde was instructed to call up all their friends and see if they had heard from him. And Madame de Lafitte insisted she should check all the local hospitals in case there had really been an accident and the police hadn't been informed.

I was left alone with old Oncle Charles. He sat slumped in his chair lost in thought, gazing at the photo.

'Who is Caroline Carr?' I asked him.

'She was an actress,' he said. 'I met her in Hollywood. She died very young. If she had lived, she would have been a great star.'

'I don't understand. Why did Michel have a photo of her?'

'Ah,' he said and paused. He leaned towards me and took my hand in his. 'He asked me if he could have it because it reminded him of someone,' he said, looking at me meaningfully.

I felt myself flushing with pleasure as he said this.

He added very softly, 'You know where he is gone, don't you, Caroline?'

I nodded and whispered back, 'Yes, but he made me promise not to tell.'

He sat back in his chair. 'It's my fault. I told him to follow his star. I filled the boy's head with dreams. I should not.'

'No. It's his father's fault, for making him study what he doesn't want.'

'Per-aps, per-aps.'

An hour or so later, Monsieur de Lafitte returned with the bike in the back of his car. Michel had left it abandoned on the side of the road at a junction that led to the motorway.

The Lafittes stood around the bike staring at it, as if hoping it could tell its story. Madame de Lafitte was still convinced that some terrible accident had happened and I was starting to feel worried as well. What if Michel had been run down by a lorry? Or had hitched a lift with some murderer or something?

The day continued with everyone jumping like mad each time the phone rang. But it was only friends and relations wondering if we'd had any news. The police didn't seem interested. It seemed sixteen-year-old boys disappeared all the time and generally were found with some girl or a load of friends who'd gone off on some binge or other. They insisted there was nothing to worry about, he'd be back before the end of the day.

I was in my room at around four in the afternoon when I heard a car swerve into the drive and come grinding to a halt outside the front door.

A dark-haired man got out of it and as he stretched to his full height I instantly recognised him. Oh-my-god! It was Marie-Christine's handsome stranger! What on earth was he doing here?

I watched as Madame de Lafitte came out to the car and greeted him affectionately. She hugged him and held him really close.

'Phillippe,' I heard her say. 'Comme je suis contente que tu es venu . . .'

Phillippe! So this was Michel's father! In the same instant I realised he was Marie-Christine's *brother* – the one whose wife had left him. So what I had seen in the café hadn't been a lovers' rendezvous at all, but simply a sister comforting her brother. How could I have got it so wrong?

When I went downstairs, the family was in the salon having a kind of conference. Michel's father came over and shook me by the hand. I looked up to find an older face but eyes very like Michel's looking at me gravely. As his eyes met mine, it felt horribly as if he could see what was going on in my head. I felt even more guilty. Should I keep the promise I'd made to Michel? Or should I go back on my word?

I sat on a chair at the table trying to follow what was going on. Monsieur de Lafitte seemed to think that Michel had gone to Paris. But if so, why hadn't he waited and gone up on the train with us and disappeared later? Matthilde seemed sure that he'd be found with some friend. Madame de Lafitte insisted that he'd gone in search of his mother.

Suddenly Michel's father turned to me and asked what I thought.

I stared down at the table. A newspaper was lying on it. As luck would have it, the headline was about the 'festival du film de Cannes'.

I felt myself blush to the roots of my hair as I looked up and caught old Oncle Charles's eye.

'Le festival de Cannes!' It's early this year,' he said thoughtfully. 'C'est ça, n'est pas, Caroline?'

All eyes turned on me.

I nodded. 'Oui.'

I hadn't really meant to give Michel away. It was a chance in a million that the newspaper should be lying there. But I felt terribly relieved that the secret was out.

Everyone started talking at once, asking questions. There didn't seem much point now in holding back the rest. So I told them what I knew. That Michel had decided to go to Cannes where he planned to play his guitar at some restaurant in order to keep himself.

Michel's father got up from his seat and grabbed his car keys as if he was going to leap into his car and take off for Cannes right away.

'Quel restaurant?' he demanded.

I racked my brain. Michel had mentioned the name but I hadn't really taken it in.

'J'ai oublié le nom,' I said.

Everyone in turn urged me to try to remember it. The shadow of a memory came back, the vaguest feeling of the word.

'I think it was something to do with French history,' I said slowly. 'To do with a palace or royalty or something.'

'Le Roi Soleil?' suggested Monsieur de Lafitte.

'Le Petit Prince?' tried Matthilde.

'Versailles?' asked Madame de Lafitte. 'Ou Fontainebleau?'

'La Pompadour?' said Matthilde.

I shook my head. They were getting me totally confused. My mind had gone blank.

'I think I'd remember it if I saw it,' I said.

'Voilà,' said Phillippe, as if there was not a moment to be lost. 'Then you must come with me. And Matthilde too.'

Madame de Lafitte said something about us being due back at school. There was a lot of discussion back and forth. But she was overruled. It was decided that Matthilde and I should go with Michel's father. In Cannes he would put us on the train back to Paris.

All of a sudden I wasn't going back to school. I was actually going to Cannes, and during the film festival. This was something to tell Jess and Angie. I had visions of sun-baked beaches, palm-shaded boulevards and glamorous yachts. Or night-time with bright lights and sleek limousines with glimpses of the stars inside. And better than any of that — I felt sure we would find Michel.

Chapter Seventeen

I hadn't realised France was such a big country. Four hours later I was still watching an endless ribbon of hard shoulder as we steamed south down the autoroute. Beyond it, the countryside was hidden behind a relentless curtain of rain. The rain had started soon after we left Les Rochers and looked set to continue. Phillippe wanted to reach Cannes before nightfall. He drove fast and tirelessly, overtaking everything in our path. Each monstrous lorry we passed doused us with a blinding wall of spray.

Matthilde and I were in the back. She'd settled into her corner with her iPod on and fallen asleep with her legs stretching uncomfortably on my side. I could hear the irritating jangle of the music from her earphones. It was icy cold in the car as Phillippe had put the air-conditioning on to keep the windscreen clear. I longed for my coat, which was in the boot with the rest of my stuff, but I didn't dare ask him to stop.

I had time to think in the car. As the windscreen wipers swept hypnotically back and forth, my mind was filled with alternative versions of what would happen when we found Michel. That was *if* we found Michel! What if we didn't? Young people did disappear. You saw posters for them on railway stations and places. I shivered at the thought. But of course we'd find him, he hadn't been gone that long. We'd find him safe and sound, playing his guitar in that restaurant. If only I could remember the name! I'd gone over it so many times in my brain, all I could remember were the names I'd rejected.

My mind then started along another tack. How would he react when we did find him? He'd know I had given him away. He'd probably be really angry and hate me for it. I stared miserably out into the gloomy landscape. Oh why did it all have to end like this?

It was about seven-thirty when we reached the turn-off for Cannes. Night was drawing in fast and it was still raining. As we approached the city, Matthilde woke up and moaned that she was hungry, so Phillippe stopped and bought us sandwiches and coffee at a service station. He ate his while driving.

We were soon winding down a long road that led between apartment blocks. I strained my eyes for signs of glamorous nightlife but all I saw was a sad-looking restaurant with a doner-kebab machine going round and round inside. Eventually, the street got busier and Phillippe turned into a wide boulevard. The traffic was at a standstill – we were caught in a traffic jam that seemed to go on for ever. All I could see were the lights of the cars ahead reflected dazzlingly in the wet tarmac. So much for the bright lights.

After an hour or so of tedious stop-start driving, we reached the seafront. Through the rain I could see the lights of yachts bobbing on the dark water. And there were palm trees, loads of them, with people huddled underneath with umbrellas, sheltering from the rain.

Phillippe drew to a stop at the side of the road and we had a sort of argument about what to do. Matthilde said we should park and walk and find our way to the old town, which was where all the restaurants were. I think she had visions of us wandering through smart restaurants, checking out the celebs till we just happened to come across Michel. But Phillippe seemed to be insisting on continuing in the car. He said something about finding a hotel for the night as the search for Michel could be a long one. I realised he was right. Cannes was a pretty big place.

There followed a nightmare two hours of searching. All the large hotels were fully booked because of the festival and we were advised to try the smaller ones. We drove through the narrow streets of the old town, often getting lost and doubling back. Each time we saw a hotel, Phillippe or Matthilde leaped out and made a dash through the rain to ask for rooms. But all gave the same response: 'Complet.' Rooms were like gold dust during the festival.

At each restaurant we passed, Phillippe paused and turned to me to see if the name rang a bell. There are hundreds and hundreds of restaurants in Cannes and most of them have names to do with the sea, like 'Le Joli Marin', 'Les Marinières', 'Le Navire' or 'Le Nautique'. They also have names of girls and flowers and songs but none of them seemed anything like the name Michel had mentioned.

By midnight, we were all feeling frayed and Matthilde was complaining of a headache. Phillippe had drawn to a stop in a square at the highest point of the old town. The rain had eased off and he got out of the car and went and leaned on some railings. Matthilde didn't want to get out; she said something about it being a stupid idea to have come to Cannes at all.

I went and joined Phillippe. He checked his mobile for the thousandth time and listened to his messages. There was still no word from Michel. He turned up his coat collar and took a packet of cigarettes out of his pocket and lit one. He stood leaning there staring down moodily, and for one heart-lurching moment he looked just like his son.

I leaned on the railings beside him.

Phillippe suddenly turned to me, saying, 'You know why Michel left?'

I nodded. 'He wants to work in films. He's really serious about it.'

Phillippe shook his head and said in a choking kind

of voice, 'And I 'ad started to make enquiries. 'Ee can go to film school if 'ee wants. As long as 'ee passes 'eez bac first.'

What a mess. If only Michel had hung on in there. I stared miserably down at the harbour. After the rain, everything seemed to glisten. The lights from the yachts cast long trails of silvery ripples over the water. In any other situation it would have been a magical view.

I left Phillippe to smoke his cigarette in peace and went for a bit of a walk to stretch my legs. In the open air, it felt welcomingly warm after the air-conditioned car. A faint steam rose off the puddles and the sound of water running down the gutters reminded me for a moment of standing on the bridge with Michel at Les Rochers.

There was music coming from around a corner. I wandered towards it and found a door leading down into a cellar restaurant. Above the door was the sign of a leaping dolphin.

Someone was playing a guitar. My skin prickled with anticipation. I checked the name of the place: 'Le Dauphin'. That was it! For some weird and incomprehensible reason, that's what the French called the heir to the throne. The Dolphin! I rushed back to Phillippe and grabbed him by the arm.

'J'ai trouvé. I think I've found it. Le Dauphin!'

Matthilde heard me and she scrambled out of the car. Together we raced down the steps of the restaurant with Phillippe hard on our heels. Our entry caused quite a stir, as smart-looking people glanced up from their meals to see two dishevelled girls in their midst. Matthilde was ahead of me and she stopped in her tracks. I followed her gaze. A guitarist was playing on a little stage at the far end of the restaurant. He had long black dreadlocks and a moustache. He was nothing like Michel.

A waiter came up and asked pointedly if he could help us. Phillippe said something about seeing the manager and explained in a low voice why we were there. We were taken into a back room beside the kitchen that smelt of rancid cooking fat. A greasy-looking man sat at a computer; he seemed annoyed to be disturbed.

From the conversation that followed, I gathered that Michel had been in there earlier in the day. But the manager had hired the other musician months ago. He'd told Michel to get lost.

Phillippe pumped him for more information, but the man just shrugged and said it wasn't his affair.

We drove despondently back through the old town, pausing whenever we saw a figure in a doorway or a likely alleyway where a boy might shelter. At one point we came across a group of people bunched around a street musician, but when we stopped we saw it was an old man with a dog on a piece of string. He was miming to a CD with a paper beaker on the ground for coins.

Now that the rain had stopped, people were coming out into the streets. I spotted a girl in a low-cut evening dress and two men in white tuxedos who might have been celebrities. We passed a cinema where people were queuing for an all-night showing and several nightclubs where we caught the low throb of music seeping out into the street. I realised sinkingly that there was little likelihood of coming across Michel by chance. It was like searching for a single face in a football crowd. He could be anywhere.

Phillippe turned back on to the seafront and we drove slowly along the promenade scanning the pavements. Cars hooted impatiently behind us. Faces loomed and faded in the beam of our headlights. Once, heart-stoppingly, we saw a boy with dark hair hanging into his eyes. Phillippe swerved to a halt. But his was nothing like the face we were searching for. At length, we reached the end of the city. We tried a last hotel on the edge of town, a dismal-looking place, but even that was full and Phillippe at last admitted defeat. It was two in the morning and we were all dead-beat. He said we'd have to sleep in the car.

He parked in a lay-by beside a beach and we ransacked the boot for all the warm clothes we could find. My coat did come in handy in the end. Mum was right, I was glad I'd brought it. I curled up underneath with a bundled-up T-shirt for a pillow.

It was a hideous night. Matthilde and I kept waking each other up each time we turned over. Some sort of party seemed to be going on in a nearby beach pavilion and there was the sound of the bass line throbbing endlessly like a dull heartbeat just loud enough to hear. Cars passed endlessly, each one throwing a blinding beam of light over us.

In the end, I must have fallen asleep, because I woke cramped and cold to the milky light of dawn. I could hear by their steady breathing that both Phillippe and Matthilde were asleep. I peered at the clock on the dashboard. It was five-thirty. Outside the sun was rising in a peachy glow over the sea. The clouds had cleared overnight and the sky was a clear unbroken pearly white. Already I could feel the faint warmth of the sun through the window.

I remembered the search of the night before and my heart turned over with a thump as I wondered where Michel was. I prayed he'd found somewhere safe and dry to sleep. I tried to get comfortable enough to go back to sleep but worry about Michel nagged at my mind. I was hungry too. It seemed ages since we'd had that sandwich from the service station. It occurred to me that if I walked back along the beach, towards the city, I'd eventually find a café or a bakery open and I could buy some croissants and maybe coffee and bring them back for the others.

Carefully, I extricated my legs from Matthilde's. She stirred but didn't wake up. I let myself out of the car, holding the handle up till the ultimate moment so the door closed silently.

Outside, the air was fresh and smelt of seaweed and some sort of spicy herb. Seagulls hovered on the wind, their harsh cries reminding me of happier seaside walks on holidays with Mum and Dad.

I made my way down the beach and doused my face in seawater. It left my skin sticky with salt but it was better than nothing. Then I set off along the shoreline. As the sun rose higher, the air grew steadily warmer. The sun glinted on the sea and I saw a yacht making out from the harbour shake out its sails and catch the wind as it headed out towards the horizon. The sunshine seemed to melt away the fears of the night before. Michel couldn't have totally dematerialised. He was here somewhere and given time we'd find him. I started to feel mindlessly optimistic. Nothing bad could happen on such a beautiful day.

I walked for about a kilometre before I came to that last hotel we'd tried. No one was awake, it was still closed up, so I continued on my way. The bay curved inwards shortly after the hotel and I came to a promontory built out into the sea forming a kind of harbour. I clambered over the rocks and found that the promenade started the other side. The first hundred metres or so had been built out from the land. It arched over the beach, making a rough kind of shelter beneath. And as is the way with such shelters, this one had attracted its usual population of the homeless and other random rough sleepers.

I shivered, wondering if Michel had spent the night in company as grim as this. I made my way past, keeping down by the water's edge, scanning the sleepers but not wanting to look too closely at the lumpy array of sleeping bags and pathetic makeshift shelters. By the look of it, most of the people were permanent residents. The overhang got narrower at the end, barely providing a shelter at all. And that's where I caught sight of a skimpy sleeping bag some way off from the others from which an arm protruded clutching – surely that was Michel's guitar?

I made my way up the beach with horrible foreboding. Empty beer and wine bottles were scattered around. Was it him? Or would some horrible bleary-eyed drunk leap out and make a grab for me? I crept closer. A tuft of tousled hair emerged from the bag – Michel's colour. And closer still – my heart was beating hard in my chest now.

It was him.

Close up, I could see he was fast asleep; his face looked crumpled and childish and none too clean. And I suddenly saw him as he really was – a boy – not so much older than me. No older, no wiser, just a kid really.

I leaned towards him and my shadow fell across his face. He woke with a start and clutched his guitar tighter. Then he saw me and a slow smile passed across his face.

'Rosbif !'

'Bonjour, Grenouille.'

He sat bolt upright and looked around him, coming out with a stream of French I didn't understand.

Then he stared at me and asked, ''Annah. What are you doing here?'

'We're all here. Me and Matthilde and your dad. We came to find you.'

He seemed to be trying to get his mind round this one.

'My father?'

I nodded. 'He was really worried about you.'

He slumped forward. ''Annah, I 'ave been such an idiot. What 'appen last night. You don't want know.'

'I can imagine.'

He shook his head. 'The man in the restaurant 'ee don't remember me. Some guy, 'ee say 'ee know some place I can play. 'Ee took me down a dark street, took a knife out. Took all my money. Took my portable. 'Ee would 'ave took my guitar too but someone come and 'ee run off.'

'Oh, Michel.'

He looked around him. At the row of bundled-up sleeping people. At the rim of rubbish on the beach. At the empty bottles strewn around on the pebbles. A slow grin spread across his face and he said out of the corner of his mouth, 'Of all the gin joints in all the towns in all the world, she 'ad to walk into mine.' It was a quote from the film we'd watched together – *Casablanca*.

We walked back together to the car after that. I was dreading what would happen when we woke his father. I thought Phillippe would be really angry, but it was worse. He cried. He just stood and hugged Michel close to him and cried. In fact I think we were all in tears. When we'd recovered, we each made loads of phone calls.

I heard Phillippe call up the de Lafittes and Marie-Christine and then Michel asked if he could have the phone. He walked off at some distance and I heard him leave a message for his mother.

When he'd finished, we all piled into the car and Phillippe drove us back into Cannes. I thought he'd head straight for Paris but he turned off the boulevard and swept into the driveway of the poshest hotel on the seafront.

The doorman seemed rather surprised by the sight of us but he made no comment. Phillippe walked in and asked where breakfast was served as if he owned the place. We were shown to a vast dining room which was all flounces and frills and tables laid with pink table-cloths and orchids. We were the only people there because it was so early and the staff were just finishing laying the tables. But there was a breakfast buffet at the far end positively heaving with food.

Matthilde and I went and tidied up in the ladies' room. They had lovely-smelling soap and soft towels and dispensers with expensive perfume in them. As I was combing my hair, I caught her eye in the mirror. She was staring at me.

'Quoi?' I asked.

'Tu sais, 'Annah. Michel, il t'aime,' she said.

I felt myself blushing to the roots and nodded. 'I know he likes me. I like him too.'

She shook her head and rolled her eyes, saying, ''Annah, I sink you are ve-ry fu-nny.'

It was an odd kind of compliment, but by the way she said it I could tell that, somewhere in the not-too-distant future, we might actually become friends. I followed her back to the breakfast room with my mind in a turmoil, wondering what she'd really meant by 'il t'aime'. Oh, how can a language be SO unspecific!

The four of us ate the most disgustingly enormous breakfast. There was everything on the buffet, from fruit and cereals, eggs done every way, sausages, bacon, muffins and pancakes – you name it. I don't think the waiters had ever seen anyone eat as much as Michel.

We all climbed back into the car feeling positively stuffed. We'd given up the idea of taking the train. Phillippe was going to drive us all back to Paris. Matthilde got in the back with me, letting Michel sit beside his father.

As we left I stared out of the window in a kind of haze. So much had happened in the last twenty-four hours it was hard to get my mind around it. And I had a few more points to add to my score of French positives and negatives.

Positives:

1) There is breakfast beyond French break-
    fast.

Negatives:

1) Words that are as horribly vague as
    'aimer', meaning both 'to like' and 'to
    love'. You'd have thought the French
    would've sorted that one out, wouldn't you?

Chapter Eighteen

The journey back to Paris seemed to take for ever. Matthilde and I shared the earphones of her iPod for most of the time and actually the music she had wasn't that bad. From time to time I took out my earphone and was hazily aware of Michel and his father talking. I couldn't understand much of what was said but I could tell by the tone of their voices that they were coming to some sort of agreement.

At midday we stopped at a service station for coffee and sandwiches. Matthilde went to tidy up in the loo and Phillippe stood outside smoking a cigarette.

'What's going on?' I whispered to Michel.

Michel leaned over into the back and said, 'Eez OK. I can go to film school. As long as I pass my bac.'

'So you *are* going back to the lycée?'

'I do not mind. As long as I know the future.'

Phillippe stubbed out his cigarette and climbed back into the car at that point. He glanced at Michel and me and gave us a sort of knowing smile. It made me go all warm inside, I don't quite know why.

It was pretty late by the time we reached Paris. We were all stiff and cramped from spending so long in the car and Phillippe looked grey with tiredness.

At last we turned into a street I recognised. Phillippe drew to a stop outside the Poiriers' apartment. Although we said we could manage our luggage, Phillippe and Michel insisted on carrying it up for us. I was glad actually. My skin felt prickly from lack of sleep. As we crammed into the lift, I was positively sagging at the knees. All I could think of was a hot shower and bed.

Marie-Christine opened the door and after she'd kissed us all she hesitated, holding the door half-open. Phillippe said something about a coffee and she shook her head.

She looked at him seriously.

'Phillippe, il y a quelqu'un ici . . .' I heard her say.

I glanced beyond her and saw a slender blonde woman in the darkness. She was silhouetted in the doorway of the salon, standing quite still. Phillippe's face went ashen pale and for a moment it was like one of those scenes in a film, when you know what's happening, although not a word is spoken. We all stood there, caught as if in a freeze-frame, as one long glance passed between them.

Michel broke the spell. He burst past his father with a cry of 'Maman'.

So this was Michel's mother. She came forward into the light. You could see that she had been a model, she was still incredible-looking. She stood hugging Michel but her eyes remained on Phillippe. He moved forward slowly at first and then more confidently. And they simply stood there staring at each other. Still not a word had been spoken but her eyes said it all. Phillippe gently put his arms around her.

I wanted to sink back into the shadows, disappear, dematerialise, not wanting to disturb this private moment. Quietly, I took my holdall and went to the room Matthilde and I had shared seemingly aeons ago. The scene behind me had dissolved into a blur of muffled words and tears. I didn't think I could take much more French emotion that day.

I closed the door, reached in my bag for my mobile and rang my mother.

'Poppet, you all right? Where are you?'

'I'm fine. I'm back at the Poiriers' in Paris. And Michel's *mother* is here!'

'Giselle's in Paris? I thought she was in the Dordogne.'

Suddenly it all fell into place.

'I think Marie-Christine must have gone to find her,' I said slowly.

'Thank god. Now maybe they can patch things up.'

'I don't understand. What was the argument about?'

'About Michel. He wanted to drop out of school. And Giselle backed him up.'

'His father and his grandfather went ballistic. That's why he ran away.'

'It was very stupid and immature of him.'

'Yes I know but . . .'

'But what?'

'Oh nothing.' There wasn't much point in trying to explain to Mum that in spite of the fact that Michel was both stupid and, I suppose, *immature*, I thought he was totally, totally irresistible.

'I hope you're not in the way. The only flight available was after lunch. I'm afraid you'll have to spend the morning in Paris.'

'That's OK.'

'It'll be lovely to have you back.'

'Ummm.'

I woke late the following day, unable for a moment to remember where I was. I stared round the room and realised I was back in Paris at the Poiriers'. And then the dream I'd been having came back to me and I realised with a jolt that I'd been dreaming in French. French! Me? I lay there going back over the dream, trying to analyse it.

I was with Michel and we were back at Les Rochers. He'd opened the door to the salon and it had been full of vintage film stars. There was some sort of party, and someone was playing that song from *Casablanca* on the piano. Matthilde came in dressed in a white dress, not the one she usually wore, but the one Marilyn Monroe had on in that famous photo of her over the hot-air vent. She asked, 'Où est Michel?' And I replied, 'Il n'est pas ici. Il est à Cannes.' And she'd flounced out saying, 'Typique!'

But Michel *was* there, he was leaning on the piano watching me. Nobody had noticed that water was flooding in through the open French windows. The water rose so fast it was like in *Titanic*. We clung on to the piano but Michel lost hold and I realised that I had to swim down to let the water out. I was swimming down and down, unable to see anything, groping in the murky water . . . When I woke up with a start.

I looked over to see if Matthilde was still asleep and found her bed was empty. Her book was lying face down on top of it.

I climbed out of bed and padded over to hers. What had she been reading all this time? Knowing her, it was bound to be something terribly grown-up and intellectual. I didn't recognise the title or the author, but the publisher was pretty familiar – *Mills and Boon*! Who would have thought! The oh-so-sophisticated Matthilde was into romances!

And then another thing occurred to me. I went back to my bed and peered underneath. The raspberry tart had gone. There was just the teeniest hint of an incriminating stain where it had been. Whoever had cleared it up, had made a really good job of it. Phew!

Marie-Christine came tapping on the bedroom door. She was carrying a glass of juice for me.

'Hannah, ma petite. You sleep so long. I did not want to wake you. I am sorry Matthilde has gone to school. And I have an important rendezvous. I feel very bad but

I cannot accompany you to the airport. But I ask Michel if he will take you. He's coming at ten to show you some sights first if that's OK?'

'That's fine,' I said, trying to hold my voice steady.

OK?!!!!! I was going to have a whole morning of Michel all to myself! In Paris!!!

That morning I discovered one fundamental thing about Paris. Paris doesn't simply have sights – it has *landmarks*.

Landmark Number 1) The Eiffel Tower. It was a bit scary in the lift and Michel slid his hand into mine and held it tight.

Landmark Number 2) A stall underneath the Eiffel Tower – where Michel said I had to choose their naffest thing, to remember him by. I chose a snowstorm with a luminous Eiffel Tower in it. I shake it every night before I go to sleep.

Landmark Number 3) A bateau-mouche – or third bench from the back on the starboard side, to be specific.

Landmark Number 4)   A snack bar on rue St
                       André des Arts — where
                       we bought hot dogs which
                       was all we could afford
                       and ate them sitting by
                       the Seine.

Landmark Number 5)   A seat on the métro
                       going out to Charles de
                       Gaulle airport. A busker
                       with an accordion was
                       actually playing 'La vie
                       en rose'.

Landmark Number 6)   The departure gate at
                       Charles de Gaulle
                       airport — where I at
                       last discovered whether
                       that kiss was for real
                       or not.

We keep in touch. We text each other a lot actually. I'll
never forget the first text he sent me.

rosbif - tu me manque terriblement.

Which I had to look up in the dictionary. It means:
'Roast Beef, I miss you terribly.'

My Own Personal Private French Vocabulary

A

aimer – eh-may – to like or *to love* – why oh why can't they have a different word for each?

au revoir – oh revwar – goodbye (literally, until I see you again – I wish!)

B

bac – short for 'baccalauréat', the French equivalent of A levels

à bientôt – a-bian-toe – see you soon (I wish even more)

baguette – ba-get – long stick of yummy French bread – or can be a French-bread sandwich with addition of ham etc.

bifteck (pronounced like it looks) – beef steak, one of the many words the French have pinched from the English

boulangerie – boo-lonje-ree – baker's – source of yummy baguettes

bisou – beezoo – kiss – as in friendly kiss not snog

C

ça y est! – that's it!

cambrioleur – phew! – burglar

chasse à cours – hunting with dogs and horses

chasse à tir – hunting with guns

cochon d'Inde – ko-shon-dand – guinea pig

cheval – she-val – horse

chevaux – shev-oh – horses – the French have to be awkward – you can't simply add an 's' to everything like we do

Club Méditerranée – a really posey kind of holiday park by the sea where everyone looks better in a bikini than you do – and knows it

concierge – kon-see-urge – fierce-looking lady who sits in a room at the entrance to an apartment block and spies on everyone going in or out

D

dauphin – dough-fan – dolphin – or heir to the French throne – don't ask me why

dérangé – day-ronge-ay – sounds like deranged but actually means 'put out' or 'fed up'

désolé – day-so-lay – sounds like desolated – but it only means 'sorry'

dis donc – dee-don – polite way to say 'oh my god'
dieu – dee-uh – god

E

escargot – es-car-go – snail or totally disgusting buttery garlicky first course
étoile – ay-twall – star
étoile filante – ay-twall fee-lon – falling star – sigh
entrée – on-tray – first course – or hallway. Just to be confusing, we use the same word for main course in English

F

fraise – fraze – strawberry (sigh)

G

glace – glas – ice cream or looking-glass
grenadine – yummy red syrup apparently made from pomegranate
grenouille – gren-oo-wee – frog (or a rather rude way to describe a French person). Happens to be one of the most difficult words to pronounce in French

H

haute cuisine – posh food that always has one rather dodgy ingredient – like foie gras or lobster claws or truffles

haute couture – clothes that are so exclusive only celebs are allowed to wear them

J

je suis ravie – NOT I am raving, as you'd expect – or ravished – but I'm delighted
je vous en prie – not at all, or it's a pleasure

L

lapin – rabbit – not to be confused with *le* pain – bread

M

malheureusement – mal-er–rurse-mon – unhappily or unfortunately
messe – mass – as in church

O

où – where
ou – or – how confusing can you get?

P

pain – bread – the best thing about France. NB le pain (m). NOT la pain!
parler – to speak – as in the most useful phrase in the language – 'Parlez vous anglais?'
Parisien/Parisienne – inhabitant of Paris – or a person we lesser mortals have to look up to with awe and respect

pas grave – nothing to do with graves – means doesn't matter

plein air – open air or free range

présenter – to introduce

pont – bridge

pouce – thumb – ma pouce – term of affection – my little one – like Tom Thumb?

Q

quatre-vingt-dix-sept – ninety-seven – only the French could have come up with such a confusing way of counting!

qu'est-ce qu'il se passe – keskisepass – convoluted way of saying such a simple thing as 'What's going on?'!

quoi – kwa – what?

quenelle – ke-nel – horribly flabby white sausage-shaped yuck made of semolina

R

ravi/ravie – pronounced like gravy without the 'g' – means delighted rather than raving

rocher – rock, pronounced as in Ferrero Rocher – yum

rosbif – roast beef (or a rather rude way to describe an English person)

S

salut – hi there

se manquer – to miss – sigh

T

tu or toi – you, singular. A kind of minefield invented by the French to test your politeness. Correct to use with people who are friends and younger than you. Positively rude to use with older or socially superior people. For people around the same age, class etc. there's a hideous waiting game to see who uses it first.

traiteur – sounds ominously like a traitor, but it's actually a person who cooks things for a deli

Tour Eiffel – Eiffel Tower – typically the French have to say it backwards

tartine – yummy sandwich of French bread spread with butter, often with a lump of plain chocolate in it at teatime – but the ultimate experience is tartine aux fraises – spread with crushed strawberries and sugar!!!

terminer – to finish – easy to remember by terminus, where buses end up

tchin-tchin – French version of cheers

V

vélo – bike

verveine – verbena – source of thin yellow tea that looks exactly like pee and probably tastes like it too

voici – here is

voilà – here is (don't ask me when and why)

vous – you (for adults or teachers or people you don't know). V. important not to be confused with tu

About the author

Chloë Rayban has written books for children of all ages, both under her pen name Chloë Rayban and her real name Carolyn Bear. *Love in Cyberia* was shortlisted for the Guardian Fiction Prize and the Carnegie Medal and her novel *Virtual Sexual Reality* was runner-up for the Guardian award. Formerly an advertising copywriter, she now writes full-time and lives in a *manoir* in France. She has two grown-up daughters.